LOVELY DAY

Diaries of Ruth Matthews Kruger; Woodcuts and Commentary by Nancy Kruger Olson

authorHOUSE®

AuthorHouse™
1663 Liberty Drive, Suite 200
Bloomington, IN 47403
www.authorhouse.com
Phone: 1-800-839-8640

First published by AuthorHouse 6/23/2009

ISBN: 978-1-4389-3863-9 (sc)

Printed in the United States of America
Bloomington, Indiana

This book is printed on acid-free paper.

DEDICATION

Ruth Matthews Kruger

"These diaries of Ruth Matthews Kruger (1958-1982) were published to provide the present and future generations an appreciation and knowledge of my mother and her influence upon the lives of those around her."

Acknowledgements

I wish to thank Alan Olson, my son, for literary expertise, computer knowledge and support regarding the publication of my mother Ruth's diaries, which I have chosen to call *Lovely Day*.

Thanks to Jerry Kruger, my brother, for his photographs and scrapbook pages, which support the diaries.

Thanks to Neil Kruger, my brother, for keeping Mother's diaries after her death and then giving them to me. His foresight has made this publication possible.

Thanks also to Jane Rantanen Hirst, Donna Rantanen Westlund and Tasha Hirst Olsonaski for providing family photographs.

Finally, I thank Sandy O'Brien for scanning and arranging the visual material and Judi Morton for editing the manuscript.

—Nancy Kruger Olson

Disclaimer

The diary entries included here are those that record world events and family history or delineate issues of health or are merely details revealing unique characteristics of an individual.

The parenthesis around a word or series of words is to note that I have added a word or series of words to clarify the entry.

The symbol ** is a notation to advise the reader that these words are my personal comments relating to the entry Mother has made.

INTRODUCTION

RUTH MATTHEWS WAS born on February 13, 1897, but we're not sure if in Beaver Dam, Wisconsin, or Dubuque, Iowa. No birth certificate or other official papers have been located to document her birth; however, the discovery of her diaries that begin in 1958 and end in 1982 gave us valuable information about the life of this wonderful woman.

Ruth never had a driver's license. She depended on either her family or friends for transportation. She reared four children to adulthood. She lived and managed her housekeeping and homemaking in an outdated house without the benefit of running water. Working in the house was inconvenient—it was poorly insulated, and it did not have central heat. The house was built around 1900 with a new part added in 1939. It was wired for electricity in 1948.

As she begins the diaries, her son Neil is in the process of taking over the 260-acre dairy operation, and her husband Orrin is in the midst of retiring.

She is the anchor for her recently widowed daughter Betty and her five young children (Mary, Donna, June, Jane, and Arne) who range in age from five to eleven. Betty is a dairy farmer, which requires hours of daily work outside. Ruth cared for one of the younger children during the week—most often it was little Arne.

Her third child Nancy is married to James B. Olson, and they live in Glenwood, Minnesota, a distance of 200 miles south. They are part of a dairy operation with his aging and ill father milking Holstein cows and raising crops.

Her youngest son Jerry is a junior in high school at Argyle, Minnesota. He will own his first parcel of land at age 17.

Ruth's notes are sparse and to the point. She reports events and seldom indulges in making judgments or showing how she feels.

Her involvement in the operation of the dairy farm (and later the corporate grain farm) becomes apparent as she reports the sale of Brown Swiss cattle, purchase of machinery, the acquisition of more land, and attendance of meetings.

She finds delight in the beauty of nature—the sighting of the "three weeks bird," the scarlet aurora borealis, the buds on the dooryard box-elder—and the bountiful harvest of cranberries, chokecherries, June-berries, and currents, all of which had to be made into jelly or jam.

Ruth was abandoned at the age of two by her strongly opinionated mother, Emma. She lived with her grandmother, Nancy Powers Matthews; grandfather, Jacob Matthews; and father, Edward (Erastus) Matthews. Grandmother Nancy expired as little Ruth said, "Now I lay me down to sleep" for her, as she sat dying in her rocking chair in her Dubuque home. The only prayer little Ruth knew was the one she recited every night before bed. The date of this event was November 18, 1903. It sets into motion the "covered wagon story."

After giving her a decent burial, Edward and Jacob sold or gave away the household goods and packed the family memorabilia in a wooden box. The census of 1900 for the City of Dubuque shows Erastus listed as a day laborer and Jacob as a lead miner. I concluded there was precious little to pack. They scrambled to complete their preparations, realizing each day that passed increased the odds of bad weather. Perhaps they owned horses and had a wagon that merely needed to be checked and made ready for the trip. They took provisions that were in Nancy's larder and started their journey—a widower missing his wife of 59 years, a young curious and enthusiastic child, and Edward who is responsible for their safety.

The trip was over 400 miles, so if they traveled 15 miles a day (stopping for hay and oats for the horses and additional provisions for themselves), the journey may have taken 30 or more days.

One of the household articles they took was Grandma's feather bed. My mother said of the old feather bed: "I remember Grandma's feather bed best because I slept on it until I was six years old. When she died we went to Deer Creek where I also had a nice warm feather bed at Aunt Deal's. My father got Grandma's feather bed and used it until he married Nellie (Peterson) and lived in Fargo. I only have a small feather bed from Grandma Kruger."

Ruth remembered (on this journey) having a turkey roasted over an open campfire—a turkey that was secured by devious means. She remembered having announced to a passing stranger, "We are having turkey!" She also remembered being scolded for giving out this information.

It seems as if they were blessed with good karma…or more likely Nancy's spirit hadn't yet finished her work and guided them safely home to Deer Creek where Aunt Deal and Christmas goose awaited them.

—Nancy Kruger Olson

Diary Entries—1958

January 4, 1958—Elling Jorgenson is burning grass in the road ditch.

January 5, 1958—It sprinkled a little…There was a rainbow.

January 6, 1958—We heard about our French farm trainee. He will be coming near the last of February. His name is Alain Salles from Montpellier Herault, France.

January 12, 1958—The Smith's from Roseau were here to look at the Karakuls (sheep).

January 14, 1958—We went to Smith's at Roseau to look at his Angus cattle to see if we will trade the Karakuls for them.
**My father was getting weary of the Karakul sheep and their offspring—the silky Persian lambs with the tight black curls. The pelts from the lambs weren't desirable since they were domestic, and also it took a lot of them to make a garment because they had to be matched. The wool of the adult sheep had lovely, long fibers and was very desirable except for its black color. It seems that all my father did was feed them and care for them without a profit.*

January 21, 1958—I joined Homemaker's club at Thorson's on the 21st.
**Mother enjoyed the Homemaker's club and never failed to note that she had been there.*

January 27, 1958—I think I saw Sputnik tonight…It was visible here at 6:15 p.m.
**Sputnik was the first unmanned capsule in space. The Russians launched it.*

January 28, 1958—Karl Nygaard was here from Saturday over night to Sunday.
**Karl was the Dairy Herd Improvement official tester. He checked the milk and kept the official record that documented each cow's butterfat production. It was a means to sell breeding stock.*

FEBRUARY 8, 1958—It was cold and windy...about -13 below. Neil and Jerry went to the short course in Warren. I didn't go to see the electronic oven.
**They must have been promoting some of the first microwave ovens.*

FEBRUARY 9, 1958—Hans Brinker is on the T.V. at 5:30 so I better hurry and get supper so I can look at it. I forgot to mention the red northern lights on Monday night.

FEBRUARY 12, 1958—We washed clothes.
**Washing clothes was a major production since all of the water had to be carried in and carried out when finished. It also had to be heated and then placed into the washing machine. The clothes had to be put through a wringer and then hung to dry on the line outside. In winter they froze dry. Ruth had a clothes dryer but did not use it all the time.*

February 15, 1958—It was -25 today...The tractor and car wouldn't start.

FEBRUARY 17, 1958—We heard that Alain Salles of France will be here on Friday.

FEBRUARY 22, 1958—Alain came today. He is a nice fellow and speaks quite good English.

FEBRUARY 23, 1958—It was very warm today...50 above.

FEBRUARY 26, 1958—It was 60 above today...We went to Selma's to get eggs.

MARCH 18, 1958—The Homemakers meeting was quite successful. All the members were here but Ethel Safranski. Betty and Arne Jr. were also here.
**Betty came to help Ruth serve lunch. Betty was a widow by this time and had winter chores plus milking to do when she got home.*

APRIL 11, 1958—Jerry is going to a teen dance at Argyle, tonight. It is the Button Hop given by the American Legion.

APRIL 28, 1958—Alain Salles spoke to the Methodist youth last night. It is very cold and stormy. It is reported to be down to zero tonight. I sent Nancy my navy tie dress. She wants to wear it to a party.
**It was made of Navy blue silk ties that the sailors wore with their dress whites. I wore it to a Federated Women's Club party.*

APRIL 29, 1958—Nancy wrote that she and Jim are expecting to be parents in October.
**I was a sixth grade instructor and was not hired again in the fall. All married, pregnant teachers were expected to silently fade away.*

JUNE 14, 1958—Alain Salles left for California on Thursday night.

JUNE 25, 1958—We got a new car on the 23rd. It is a Plymouth and very nifty looking.

JULY 1, 1958—On Friday we all took a ride in the new car. We went to Minto, North Dakota and bought a small Allis Chalmers combine for the beans.

JULY 30, 1958—The Marshall county fair was very well attended. There was such a large crowd they couldn't all get into the grandstand. Delmar Hagen and his (Red River) ox cart and Governor (Orville) Freeman were entertaining—telling jokes and making small talk.

AUGUST 10, 1958—Jim and Nancy are building their house. It has been as high as 95 above in the shade.
**The house was a model from Wadena Sawmills and came with the lumber and blueprints in a package and cost $4,750. The finished total was about $10,000.*

AUGUST 19, 1958—Jim had to have surgery for a ruptured hernia. Pa's name is in the "Who's Who in Minnesota" book for 1958. Neil sold 2000 bushels of wheat to the elevator for $1.90 a bushel.
**Jim was doing some heavy lifting and shoveling at the site of the new house when he experienced a strangulated hernia.*

SEPTEMBER 26, 1958—We are all done with the combining and silo filling. Selma and Willie helped me some with the work.
**It was customary to serve an extra nice lunch such as sandwiches, bars, apple pie or cake. The noon meal was extensive with a roast, potatoes, gravy, a salad, and dessert. Selma and Willie lived about a mile away near the Schey country school.*

SEPTEMBER 28, 1958—We went to Deer Creek on the 17th to see Myrtle Conner. We also drove by the old farm at Deer Creek. The leaves are very pretty. The woodbine and blackhaws are especially nice because they are bright red.
**The farm was my grandfather Kruger's. It had a brick house and a barn.*

OCTOBER 8, 1958—Nancy and Jim have moved to their new house. We sent the baby's gift off today. They expect it soon.
**This was Mark, born October 30, 1958.*

NOVEMBER 23, 1958—This is an old time blizzard. Carl Nygaard, the DHIA tester, had to stay over today and perhaps tomorrow. Betty phoned saying that she can't come for Thanksgiving. The kids got over the rabies shots alright.
**They had played with puppies that had been near a rabid skunk.*

NOVEMBER 27, 1958—It is Thanksgiving Day. The cars can go now, but no milk truck or mail. We are alone for dinner. We have a turkey and the trimmings.

DECEMBER 15, 1958—Arne has been here over a week. He has a bad cold.

DECEMBER 21, 1958—Betty got Arne on Saturday, and brought down gifts. She thinks she won't be here at Christmas.

December 26, 1958—Betty and family and Selma were here for dinner. Neil was quite sick and fainted today. He is better tonight. Goodbye 1958…It was a good year. Many things took place. Crops were good. We bought new land for Jerry and Alain (Salles) was here from France.

Diary Entries—1959

January 4, 1959—We went to Brosdahl's in the afternoon. Hans has no mind left. I hope I never get that way.
**Mother had little to worry about in this instance. We wrote letters until the day she died. She became more and more lucid as her body deteriorated.*

January 5, 1959—A nice day. It was 22 below zero. We washed clothes.

February 19, 1959—My birthday has come and gone. I am 62 years young or old. We got a picture of Nancy and Mark. He is cute. It was a bad stormy day so Betty left for home early. Arne is here for two weeks. He and I went to Homemakers at Don Whitlow's in Argyle.

February 20, 1959—The men saw the first skylarks today!

March 3, 1959—Betty didn't get Arne yet.

March 12, 1959—Delaquis from Notre Dame, Canada, were here today and bought a bull.

April 2, 1959—Neil went to the (border) with a bull for Delaquis. He made the trip trouble free.

April 15, 1959—Jerry saw Nancy and baby Mark as the bus stopped in Glenwood. He is the first (of us) to see the baby (Mark).

April 19, 1959—Neil, Bob Barr and Jim Nichols left for Dickenson, North Dakota and Sedily, Montana at 3:30 a.m. to deliver two bull calves.

April 21, 1959—This is the first day Neil went to seed. It is dry and windy...no rain in sight.

MAY 1, 1959—Jerry and I went to Nancy's in Glenwood. Mark is cute. He has blue eyes and brown hair and tries to creep.

MAY 12, 1959—Jerry took Bonnie Rokke to the prom and got in at 4:30 A.M. exhausted. I guess they had a good time and no accidents.

MAY 31, 1959—Betty came down for Jerry's graduation exercises. Betty gave him Arne Sr.'s deer rifle. Uncle Jerry sent him a $50 check.

JUNE 12, 1959—We all went to Dairy Day (at Thief River Falls). Jerry got the champion ribbon but can't take the trip to Waterloo, Iowa. He is the reserve.

JUNE 28, 1959—We went to Willis Grochow's wedding last night at Newfolden. We had a flat tire as we had to take the old car. Jerry bent the fender on the new one when he came from Winnipeg on Wednesday.

AUGUST 27, 1959—Betty was here today and got some sweet corn. She got the kids clothes for school. She had a hard time getting Arne to wear his. I have been busy canning and pickling. Jerry leaves for the State fair next Friday and will go to N.D.A.C. (North Dakota Agricultural College) from there. It had been raining every day so they can't harvest much. Betty had too much rain also and it spoiled the clover seed.

OCTOBER 13, 1959—Jerry came home on Friday and will leave on Monday with the car…He likes it there.

OCTOBER 15, 1959—The weather was fierce—raining and snowing. Hans Brosdahl was buried today. We went to the funeral. Neil was a pallbearer. A miserable day.

OCTOBER 16, 1959—Neil and I went to Nancy's on October 10th. Mark doesn't walk alone yet. He is cute but was afraid of me.

OCTOBER 23, 1959—I got a letter from Nancy—she says Mark is walking alone some now. He gets up in the middle of the floor.

OCTOBER 24, 1959—We had the first snowfall today. They are picking corn yet and are on the last load. We had good corn and sold a lot of it and have a lot for ourselves (to feed the cows).

OCTOBER 25, 1959—Harry Ranstrom came to work on October 25th. He is capable and friendly. **With Jerry gone they needed another pair of hands even though harvest was completed.*

DECEMBER 13, 1959—Nancy named her baby Ruth Lynn. She was born on December 10th. **These few words do not accurately express the joy my mother experienced having a Grandchild named for her. She went shopping and purchased a pink nylon dress for her granddaughter that was trimmed with lace and had a pink under slip.*

Pumpkins - 2008

DIARY ENTRIES—1960

JANUARY 17, 1960—Pa is 65 years old now. (It was his birthday on the 16ᵗʰ). Jerry was home over the weekend to fill out his draft questionnaire.

FEBRUARY 1, 1960—Neil and I went to church. Mrs. Gunnerson gave us news of Alain Salles. He is in Algeria and was in the hospital over the holidays.

FEBRUARY 3, 1960—It is raining—a dismal and dark afternoon. Neil had to go to Crookston to give blood for Mrs. Fred Olson of Argyle. He isn't back yet.

MARCH 16, 1960—Neil complains a lot…he doesn't feel well.

MARCH 27, 1960—We went to Grand Forks on Thursday to see about Orrin's social security. The man was pleasant and accepted things very well.

APRIL 30, 1960—Neil and I went to Nancy's and came home on Sunday. The baby (Ruth) is cute and looks something like Nancy. Mark has changed his looks and is thinner. We had a good trip.

JUNE 12, 1960—Nancy, Jim, Mark and Ruth were up last weekend. Uncle Jerry was here from Wednesday and left on Sunday. Jim Olson and Pa took him back to Grand Forks to catch the plane.
**This is the time that our daughter Ruth slept in the vintage wicker baby buggy. Her tiny hand became uncovered during the night, and when I picked her up in the morning it was ice cold.

JULY 11, 1960—The Brown Swiss picnic was here at the farm. There were about seventy-five people (in attendance).

July 31, 1960—We had a lot of raspberries to eat and I canned thirty quarts of June berries.
**June berries are a sweet fruit (smaller than a blueberry) that grow on trees several feet tall. In Canada they are called Saskatoon berries.*

September 4, 1960—I fell on my arm and it hurt it quite badly. It was two weeks or more ago. It is almost healed now.

September 18, 1960—We went to Alf Alden's threshing bee at Oslo, Minnesota. There were lots of old steam tractors and other antiques.
**My father threshed for the neighbors and himself. He used gas-powered machines rather than steam tractors.*

October 4, 1960—It is a nice warm day—above 90 above. The leaves are beautiful red, brown and yellow. Pa is mowing the lawn. I picked a big bouquet of sweet peas today and canned tomatoes—about 20 quarts.

November 28, 1960—Nancy, Jim, Mark and Ruth came up on Saturday and left on Sunday. We had our Thanksgiving dinner on Sunday. Betty and kids were here. Jerry also was home.

DIARY ENTRIES—1961

JANUARY 10, 1961—Jerry brought Richard Tangen home with him last weekend. He is a nice kid and is from Hawley.
**As fate would have it, this particular person was the father of Richelle Tangen who married Jerry's son, Garth Kruger, in 2006.*

FEBRUARY 12, 1961—Betty and family were here yesterday. Betty acts hard up and wants to get some seed from Neil if she plants a crop.

MARCH 1, 1961—Jerry is home and will skip spring term to help with the spring work. Pa made a statement about the damage the ducks did to her crops. She will take it to the legislature on Wednesday for a claim of $6,000.
**Betty's land bordered the Mud Lake Wildlife refuge.*

MARCH 12, 1961—Tomorrow is John Deere day. We will most likely go.
**As the "three weeks bird" was most certainly a sign of spring, so too was the coming of John Deere Day. Young farm boys were allowed to skip school on that day to participate in the activities, movies and free meal.*

MARCH 25, 1961—Neil was in the hospital from Sunday until Wednesday afternoon. It is his nerves. He has to go to Fargo to see a specialist.

APRIL 9, 1961—We are taking the sheep (Karakuls) to Betty's place tomorrow. Pa gave them to her.
**It was Betty's idea to raise them. They are beautiful, exotic creatures with the most exquisite lambs. Their wool was equally lovely with especially long fibers; however, the wool was docked in price because of its dark color, and for this reason the sheep were not desirable. Weavers would have utilized it, but at that time my father didn't know any of these artisans. Also, the baby lambs were killed for their pelts. These were called Persian lambs, and their fur was used to make coats. My father developed an aversion—an extreme distaste—to killing healthy, newborn lambs to get their fur. So, he gave them to Betty to raise.*

June 13, 1961—Nancy, Jim and family were here over the weekend. We went to the Old Mill on Sunday. Betty came there too. Nancy is expecting in October.
**This would be my last pregnancy.*

June 20, 1961—The Marshall County fair begins tomorrow. Betty is showing the cattle and the girls have demonstrations. I will try to go one day. Jerry and Neil are also showing Brown Swiss.

July 24, 1961—The Fair was very good. I took the old civil war letters to be displayed.
**These letters were in a wooden box that was brought by Jacob, Ed, and Ruth when they traveled by covered wagon from Dubuque to Deer Creek in November of 1903.*

August 20, 1961—The men looked at Betty's flax and will combine it this fall.

August 28, 1961—Betty and Jerry went to the State Fair on Sunday. Jerry went to show our Brown Swiss cows and Betty to show Mary's calf.

September 17, 1961—Neil got the bulk milk tank set up and ready to use yesterday. It is very handy.

October 13, 1961—Betty has duck hunters. She gets $2.50 per person per shooting hours.

October 22, 1961—Betty is having her sale October 31. She is not selling the cows. Nancy's boy, Alan Matthew, was born on Wednesday—the day of Jim's Aunt Agnes' funeral. He weighed 9 pounds ½ ounce. I hope it doesn't rain or snow for Betty's sale tomorrow.

November 3, 1961—We were at Betty's auction sale. It was a big one. She said it was about $4,000.

Diary Entries—1962

JANUARY 8, 1962—It is very stormy—almost a blizzard. Pa was to the doctor on Thursday. He told him to take his pills. Nancy says Alan has his Grandfather Kruger's nose and chin. I sent Nancy a box of rags for her braided rug.
**I was braiding a wool rug but never finished it.*

FEBRUARY 2, 1962—I was to the hospital on Monday to see Mrs. Brosdahl (Edna). She has milk leg and arthritis…but seemed cheerful.
**I have no concept as to what "milk leg" might be.*

FEBRUARY 5, 1962—We had a terrific blizzard yesterday but not the doomsday one like predicted. Saturday afternoon at the short course in Warren, a woman from Grand Forks told the ladies how to fix wild game with wine and beer. It tasted good but I don't cook with wine. I gave the recipes to Betty.
**My mother abstained from all spirits and raised me as a teetotaler.*

FEBRUARY 20, 1962—We saw John Glenn go into orbit today. It was very thrilling.
**We did not own a television until possibly 1963 or 1964. We bought one from Jerry Melby who had an extra set. Mark was either five or six years old.*

MARCH 11, 1962—Our new hired man Donald Hamilton came today. Jerry went back to Fargo for his third quarter. Pa was sick yesterday with his heart.

MARCH 18, 1962—Pa saw a three weeks bird yesterday.
**Mother has used this term several times. It was the harbinger of spring-like weather.*

APRIL 2, 1962—Betty has twenty-five Karakul lambs and ten bottle lambs. Neil bought an Allis tractor at Nichols. It is a D-17 and looks like new. He drove it home.

MAY 1, 1962—Wally gave us an estimate on digging the trench for the bathroom septic tank system.
**This is an indication that a bathroom with running water was in the works.*

MAY 7, 1962—We moved Jerry's bed to the basement, as he (Orrin) wants this space for the bathroom. We expect someone to start on it tomorrow.
**The basement in that house was warm, but primitive. It had rough, poured concrete walls and floors. The entire house was built for $1,300 in 1939. I recall how happy I was for my parents to have a bathroom with running water and a stool that flushed. These days we would admire them for thinking 'Green,' not polluting the ground water. But when you are in your mid to later sixties, nature tends to call much more often—requiring facilities close at hand.*

MAY 11, 1962—Deschene worked on the bathroom this week. He put in the partition and tile and floor covering. It looks very well.

MAY 27, 1962—We got our bathroom fixtures in and are waiting for the digging before we can use it.

JUNE 16, 1962—Last weekend Jim and Nancy and children were here.
**I was so impressed with the new bathroom.*

AUGUST 26, 1962—It is hot and dry—about 90 above in the shade. They are combining. The crops are good. The wheat is 35 bushels an acre…some of it is going 30 bushels an acre. Betty picked up June and left little Arne.
**June, Ruth's granddaughter, was old enough to be a great help.*

SEPTEMBER 23, 1962—Jerry gets to go to Waterloo, Iowa (to the Dairy Cattle Congress). He will be gone nine days and will visit fifteen places. Betty and Mary were here awhile this afternoon. Betty wanted to see Pa and Neil about borrowing a tractor and plow.

SEPTEMBER 30, 1962—The barn is almost done.
**Neil is building a new Grade-A dairy barn.*

OCTOBER 15, 1962—Swenson's are working on the furnace today. I guess they will finish it up.
**Previous to this they had a space heater in the old part of the house. My dad hand carried the fuel for the oil-burner into the living room. The upstairs was not heated at all, and there were no registers in the floor. In the coldest weather, Mother opened the door to the upstairs allowing the heat to rise.*

OCTOBER 23, 1962—The furnace works good and (is) sure a nice thing. It looks like war! The United States has blockaded Cuba. Castro says there is the greatest danger of war since World War II.
**This was known as the "Cuban Missile Crisis." This is when people built bomb shelters in their basements and stocked them with enough supplies of food and water to last several months. My kids wore bracelets on their tiny wrists so they'd be identified if killed while away at school. This is when kids learned to duck under their desks and cover their heads with their hands as a means of protection from the bomb!*

OCTOBER (?), 1962—The new dairy barn is progressing slowly.

DECEMBER 23, 1962—We had a bad blizzard yesterday. Two people froze to death. It was Mrs. Hudson and her daughter.

Diary Entries—1963

January 29, 1963—Betty was down and got calves. Neil is going Grade-A soon.

January 31, 1963—We were up to Betty's yesterday. Neil traded milkers with her. He goes on Grade A tomorrow.
**Grade-A milk had to meet certain requirements in the dairy setup, and creameries paid a higher premium for the milk.*

February 27, 1963—Pa and I got the Valley Farmer and Homemaker Award at Crookston last Thursday. Betty took us (to the banquet).
**This was part of the Crookston Winter Shows.*

March 8, 1963—We got our photograph of those who were honored. It is good.

March 30, 1963—It is very warm—76 above. They will start in the field this week.

April 4, 1963—Today we have a blizzard.

April 14, 1963—This is Easter Sunday. It is about 80 above.

May 2, 1963—The men are half done seeding and will finish up out east at noon. It is very windy and dusty.

May 19, 1963—It snowed so the ground and trees were white.

May 26, 1963—Pa and Neil left for Columbus, Ohio, and will stop several places to see Brown Swiss. They will also stop at Beaver Dam, Wisconsin, to see Virgil Knaup (Dad's cousin), and Urbana, Illinois, to see Uncle Jerry and Eri and to see Nancy and Jim at Glenwood.

SEPTEMBER 28, 1963—Orrin had a prostate operation a month ago. He has a tube in him yet. He will go to Grand Forks tomorrow to see about it. He hasn't been too happy with the catheter. It is a nuisance.

SEPTEMBER 30, 1963—We had our first real frost on the 28th of September.

OCTOBER 27, 1963—Jerry went to Nancy's pheasant hunting and brought home two pheasants. We had one last Sunday. It was good...nice and tender. It is still warm and sunny. Pa and I sat outdoors both today and yesterday. Pa got the storm windows all on.
**The storm windows came off in the spring and were put back on in the fall. Separate screens replaced the storm windows in the summer.*

NOVEMBER 24, 1963—President Kennedy was shot (in Dallas) on November 22. His supposed assassin was shot today as he was being moved to the county jail in Dallas, Texas. That is where Kennedy was shot riding in a motorcade. The funeral for Kennedy is tomorrow, November 25th.

DECEMBER 7, 1963—Nancy, Jim, and their children; Betty and family and Jerry were home for Thanksgiving. Nancy and Jim left on Saturday.
**I don't remember this trip. I suppose Jim's brothers were still available to help milk the cows. His dad was seriously ill with heart disease.*

DECEMBER (?), 1963—Jerry went on the judging team at the cattle show.

DECEMBER 16, 1963—We've had two blizzards in about a week. Neil has (had) a toothache and a bad cold now for about two weeks. We don't have a Christmas tree yet. There are three fresh cows so plenty of work for Pa and Neil.
**A fresh cow is one that has recently had a calf.*

DECEMBER 26, 1963—We were alone on Christmas except for Jerry and Neil. Betty and family came on Monday and brought gifts.
**I know how this feels since this has been the norm for many years.*

DECEMBER 29, 1963—We had Selma and Willie over for dinner.
**This year, I had Howard and Larry over before Christmas. Howard is a friend from the humane society, and Larry is Jim's long time fishing partner.*

Jack in the Pulpit - 2007

Diary Entries—1964

January 7, 1964—Jerry left for Fargo on Sunday. We hated to see him leave after being home for Christmas vacation. He has two months left before he graduates.
**I still hate to see my kids leave. After all these years I should be accustomed to the routine, but I always experience a sense of loss.

February 5, 1964—They are hauling barley to Grand Forks for .90 cents a bushel.

February 14, 1964—Pa gave me a Helbros wrist watch for my birthday.
**Her birthday was February 13, 1897.

March 15, 1964—Jerry is home and has finished college.

April 22, 1964—They started in the field. It is wet and rainy.

April 30, 1964—I helped Pa plant peas today. It is wet in the garden.

June 1, 1964—I hurt my hands. The lawn chair arms collapsed on them and cut them. I had to have five stitches in each one. A hard frost killed lots of the plants in the garden.

June 14, 1964—Jerry, Neil, Pa and I took Jane (Rantanen) to Ulen on Sunday. Nancy met us there and took her home to help baby sit the kids. She will stay about a month while Nancy goes to summer school at the University of Minnesota at Morris.
**This is the summer I took Shakespeare and got an A in the class. To pay Jane, I sewed several articles of clothing for her.

August 13, 1964—We all went to Betty's last night. Betty was plowing her diverted acres.
**Diverted acres refers to a government program.

SEPTEMBER 6, 1964—Jerry got put in class C2 which is agricultural deferment.
*This was a defining event for Jerry. My father was sixty-nine at the time and not physically able to continue working as in prior years.

SEPTEMBER 7, 1964—Nancy and Jim came up last Saturday and got here at 1:30 P.M. and left on Sunday about 4 P.M. Nancy brought apples from their orchard...they were real nice.
*As we arrived at the farm, my parents stood waiting—framed by the doorway. It had such a visual impact on me, and demonstrated how eagerly they awaited our coming. Each time they looked older. It was a touching scene and is a fine memory.

OCTOBER 13, 1964—Pa is going to Betty's hunting tomorrow morning.
*Dad is savoring retirement.

OCTOBER 16, 1964—Neil got hurt by a bull at Nowaskis on Wednesday. He had two fractured ribs and stitches in his hand. The bull got Neil down and butted him.
*Farmers began to use artificial insemination in the early 1970s. It was much safer and provided the best bloodlines available without the danger involved with keeping a bull.

OCTOBER 20, 1964—Neil is able to work today. I am glad.

NOVEMBER 8, 1964—It is warm and sunny. Selma and Willie are coming over for supper and to look at the colored television.
*The Olson's did the same thing—supper and television.

NOVEMBER 18, 1964—Neil and Bill Grochow have gone to the Twin Cities to (the) Grain Terminal Association Convention.

NOVEMBER 23, 1964—Neil got home on Friday night. Nancy sent apples and two pheasants.
*This is when Neil and Bill Grochow stopped at our house on their way back. I prepared a pheasant in a brown paper bag. It was tender, moist, and so delicious.

Diary Entries—1965

January 25, 1965—The Homemakers turned out quite well. There were eight women here besides me. They worked on dish towels.

February 3, 1965—Jerry got a job being a substitute instructor in Agriculture at Karlstad. It will be for a month or more.

February 17, 1965—Brosdahl's were here on Sunday evening to look at television.
**It was Walt Disney at 6 P.M., Jack Benny at 7 P.M., and Ed Sullivan at 8 P.M.*

February 28, 1965—We had four Canadians here for over night last week. It was two men and two women. The men wanted to buy cattle. They were from Saskatchewan—about 500 miles from here.

March 26, 1965—Jerry went to Fargo to see about getting his assistantship at U.N.D.A.C. (Now N.D.S.U.).

April 6, 1965—Jerry got on the N.F.O. (National Farmer's Organization) 'Grain Bargaining Board' last night at Newfolden.

April 11, 1965—Palm Sunday. It is dreary and cloudy. We went to look at the water. It looks like a lake on the fields. Also, the river is almost to the bridge and the ditches are almost full of water in places.
**As kids we loved the water. One spring when the ditches were full, I commandeered my Mother's galvanized washtub and used it to set sail on the river of water that was beside our house. It seemed like fun to me, a small child of six or seven. My mother quickly grasped at the inherent danger and ordered me to stop at once.*

April 14, 1965—It is bad about every place. Marville Magnusson had about forty acres underwater near his house. Crookston evacuated 1500 people. We looked at the flood again Monday night. It is over the road past Gustafson's and the bridge is impassible at Baggas's. They moved their cattle to Moe's.
**This was across the road.*

April 19, 1965—Pa and I gave Mary $50 for a graduation gift. The kids were here for Easter—all but Betty. Mary brought a hot-dish, salad and doughnuts. She had on her new dress for Easter and graduation. It is white with a red rose across the bodice. It is very pretty.

April 21, 1965—Pa and Neil took 9 head of cattle to Greer at Dominican City, Canada, yesterday.

April 22, 1965—Neil, Betty and Donna went to Sundown, Canada today to the Ukrainian Easter Sunday services.
**My father would comment that having an open border between the United States and Canada was to be appreciated because it wouldn't last.*

April 30, 1965—Pa planted early garden yesterday and today. I planted glads (gladiolas) and sweet peas today.
**This poem reflects my father's sentiments almost as if he wrote it:*

> This used to be among my prayers:
> A piece of land not so very large,
> Which would contain a garden,
> And near the spring of ever flowing water,
> And beyond these a bit of wood…
>   —Horace 65-8 B.C.

May 16, 1965—Lovely day. We went to church with Pa. The trees are green and the tulips are out and the garden is coming up.

May 27, 1965—We went to Mary's graduation and came home quick because the Canadians were here to get the cows and calf. Betty and Neil went along to the border. They were too goofy to go alone.

June 16, 1965—Neil has gone to Washington D.C. as a Farmer's Union delegate. He flew from Minneapolis and went with a group from Oklee. Jerry is at Betty's helping plant the crops. Uncle Jerry comes on June 25th. He wants to go to Wadena and to Bemidji to fish.

July 3, 1965—Last weekend on Sunday morning Pa, Jerry Sr., and Jerry Jr. went to Wadena. Nancy, Jim and family came to Wadena and they had a picnic at Leaf Lake.

July 12, 1965—Pa bought a Commodore Rambler from Clifford Jorgenson. It has seat belts in it! We were up to Betty's yesterday. She was making hay. We fixed lots of peas, beans and currents this week.

AUGUST 5, 1965—Our road is mostly dug up past here…so we have to go north but may not be able to go that way soon. They are also making a road on the town-line so we can't go out of here to the west either. We went to church on Sunday. Mrs. Gunnerson told us that Alain Salles and his mother drove to Turkey to see his sister and had a bad accident. The car was demolished but they weren't hurt.

AUGUST 14, 1965—It was 98 above yesterday. It was 100 in Crookston. It is very dry and dusty. The crops are very good. Selma picked chokecherries last Thursday. June helped her.
*My parents did not have air-conditioning, only electric fans.

AUGUST 20, 1965—Harry Kennedy's funeral was this afternoon at (?). I thought Neil should combine wheat if he could. We sent a big bouquet of mums and I wrote Madge a letter.
*This comes under the heading of "Making hay while the sun shines." Farming first, anything else second.

AUGUST 21, 1965—I made cranberry jelly and jam.
*It was from wild high bush cranberries and was sinfully delicious.

AUGUST 29, 1965—Nancy, Jim and children were here last Saturday and went home on Sunday. Jim looked at the new roads, saw the colored television and listened to Jerry's stereo record player. Jim took home new potatoes, cranberries and melons.

SEPTEMBER 17, 1965—It is still cold and rainy so they can't combine. There has been lots of snow in North Dakota, Canada, Montana, and Nebraska. There were thirteen inches of snow in Nebraska and four to five in parts of North Dakota.

OCTOBER 14, 1965—It was a lovely day. Neil and Jerry finished combining all but the wheat out east.

OCTOBER 23, 1965—Pa and Neil hauled three truckloads of hay up to Betty's place.

NOVEMBER 5, 1965—The boys finished up combining today out east. November 5th is the latest date ever for them to combine.

NOVEMBER 10, 1965—Nancy asked Pa, Betty, and I to come there for Thanksgiving dinner. It has snowed so much we are afraid to go far away since it might become a blizzard.

DECEMBER 12, 1965—Jerry has gone to Fargo this weekend to see Ginny. He bought himself a Polaroid camera. Mary has gone to Harp's to work for two or three weeks. Mrs. Harp is in the hospital.

DECEMBER 29, 1965—Jerry has gone to (Ginny) Erickson's for the New Year's at Battle Lake.

Diary Entries—1966

January 1, 1966—Harp's brought Mary back from Canada today. His two girls were along. Betty, June and Jane were with her. There were seven extra we weren't expecting for dinner in addition to Gene and Marlene Jorgenson.

January 16, 1966—Jerry has been cleaning up after the blizzard. There are mountains of snow all around so I can't see the barn. Betty was here. Her cows have to eat straw or starve. She can't get at the hay.
Jerry took Neil to the hospital on January 11th with a bad heart attack. He still has spells and had one just before we got there this morning so we couldn't talk much. The doctor says he has a lot of heart damage so may be in the hospital a long time.
**Later on Neil came to realize that these episodes that the doctors called "heart attacks" were in reality stress-induced hypoglycemia, which have some of the same symptoms as a heart attack—dizziness and a racing heart.*

January 26, 1966—Jerry brought Neil home from the hospital today. He seems not too bad and (we) hope he will keep quiet. (Richard) Tangen came yesterday. He just got back from Viet Nam about a week ago. He is glad to be alive. It is stormy today but not so cold.
**The ultimate irony was that Richard was later killed in a farm related accident. Farming was more deadly than the war.*

February 15, 1966—Richard left for home today. I hated to see him go. He was nice to have around. We liked him. Betty came on Valentine's Day. She was shook up because Mary joined the W.A.A.C.S. She leaves in August.
Pa is all worn out from the cows and calves. Neil is getting better. He went to the barn and back today and didn't get tired. Neil was at the Dr. on Friday. He said he should go to the clinic in Grand Forks.

March 3, 1966—It is a very bad blizzard today and the wind is raging about and there are big drifts of snow between here and the gate. It is one of the worst blizzards I've ever seen. Neil can't go to Grand Forks tomorrow. There is no travel on any roads.

April 4, 1966—The flood is on full blast. Jerry had to help Einar Baggas move out of the house. It looks as if the bridge will over flow with water.
**It is very flat in Marshall County; therefore, when the snow melts the water has no place to go and floods the land. The drop in elevation per mile is imperceptible as one goes towards the Red River. The Red River flowing north into Canada further complicates the problem.*

April 12, 1966—Donna, Jane and June came for Easter Dinner. Donna drove since she has her driver's license. She brought a nice salad, eggs and daffodils. Betty hauled hay from our stack almost every day since she hasn't any of her own.

May 4, 1966—Jerry and Dale Brosdahl are going in the field for the first time today. I hope they don't get stuck.

May 25, 1966—Betty was here this morning and wants Pa to help her pay her taxes.

June 15, 1966—Jerry went fishing to Richard Tangen's at Hawley. The grain is up nicely. It is still rainy and windy. June has been here over a week. We are cleaning house. Pa's tulips are beautiful.

June 21, 1966—Pa, Neil and I were to Nancy's last Saturday the 18th and came home on the 19th. Pa went fishing with Jim, his Dad and his brother at Lake Minnewaska. He got some small fish. We stopped at Richville and visited Sunberg's, Klein's, and Mielkes' Store. The town is a ghost town.
**My mother and dad owned a general store at Richville from 1919-1930. They traded the store for the farm in Marshall County.*

July 10, 1966—We were to Betty's for the Brown Swiss picnic on the 3rd of July. It was a nice day. Jim's father, Mort Olson, is in the hospital at Glenwood.

August 9, 1966—Ginny Erickson, her brother, Charles, and wife, Yvonne, of Maine Township Ottertail County were here on Sunday. They were all nice and very interesting.

THE OTHER HALF OF 1966 IS MISSING. WE PICK UP IN JANUARY 1967.

Corn - 2008

Diary Entries—1967

January 17, 1967—Pierre Delaquis and two sons were here today. He bought a bull to be delivered for $300.

January 19, 1967—We heard from Nancy. She writes that Uncle Jerry recommends that Pa and I should go to Hawaii for our 50th wedding anniversary.
**My parents' 50th wedding anniversary would be on September 2, 1967.*

January 20, 1967—Nancy says that Jim rented his dad's place for the next year. Jim's dad is very ill.

January 29, 1967—Three prominent astronauts burned in their rocket. They were buried today. They were Grissom, White and Chaffee.

February 1, 1967—I am glad January is gone. It was a miserable month.

February 7, 1967—Nancy writes that Jim bought his dad's farm and house. I don't know what he paid for it.
**I was teaching kindergarten at Villard on the day the papers were signed.*

February 12, 1967—I celebrated my seventieth birthday. We had chicken and corn on the cob. We wash clothes tomorrow. It was -26 yesterday.

February 16, 1967—Argyle has no water in the town. The pipes have broken. Dale Brosdahl got water here.

February 19, 1967—June was championship sheep judge at the Crookston winter shows.

FEBRUARY 20, 1967—Duray was here today and wants to sell his land to the boys for $14,000 with $8,000 down.

FEBRUARY 24, 1967—Neil and Jerry bought the Duray land of 160 acres for $8,000 down and rented the other 160 acres for $8 an acre.

MARCH 17, 1967—I have only NFO on the radio and no St. Patrick's Day music. The milk withholding started yesterday. The boys held theirs for $1.00 per 100 weight.

MARCH 21, 1967—The NFO (National Farmer's Organization) dumped milk in Argyle on Tuesday the 21st.

MARCH 24, 1967—The NFO is still holding milk and having meetings.

MARCH 25, 1967—Jerry and the NFO-ers were around all day getting people to send telegrams to President Johnson and Governor Levander about raising the price of milk to $1.00 per 100 weight.

MARCH 27, 1967—All is peaceful with the NFO but guess they are losing out. Jerry and Dale (Brosdahl) picketed for milk holding at E. Grand Forks last night until midnight.

MARCH 31, 1967—Brooks picks up the milk with the truck. The strike is over. Massey won't take them back for awhile.
**Neil recalls that he had to eat humble pie—speaking both for himself and the others involved—to be taken back into Massey's fold.*

APRIL 10, 1967—Neil sold a cow to Delacroix for $625.

APRIL 11, 1967—Massey will take Neil back again on Thursday.

APRIL 17, 1967—It snowed about ten or twelve inches last night. No travel (was) advised and no school. Also, there was thunder and lightning last night.

APRIL 22, 1967—The people from South Dakota bought Mary's cow for $500 delivered.

APRIL 24, 1967—Pa and I picked out a new covering for the kitchen floor. Pa and I also looked at washing machines. We need a new one badly.

APRIL 27, 1967—Orrin and I went to Argyle to the veterans of World War I banquet at the American Legion.

APRIL 28, 1967—Jerry speaks in church (Methodist) tomorrow on the National Farmer's Organization. L.L. Daby will talk for the (John) Bircher's. Both speeches promise to be very interesting. Jerry went to Fargo to get Ginny to hear his speech at the church.

MAY 1, 1967—There were tornadoes in southern Minnesota with rain and snow here. It is discouraging weather (for farming).

MAY 2, 1967—Heard from Nancy. They have 70 acres planted already. Mark works also.

MAY 5, 1967—Betty took Mary's cow to South Dakota yesterday. Jerry went to Fargo to judge cattle at N.D.A.C.

MAY 6, 1967—Dushek came on Tuesday to buy two cows…so Betty has some money now.

MAY 7, 1967—Pa, Jerry and I went east and looked at Jerry's new land. We also saw the swamp, which looks wet and ducks live there.

MAY 11, 1967—Pa and I sat outside in our lawn chairs and later took a little drive to look at the fields.

MAY 13, 1967—Neil has one hundred acres seeded so far. Jerry and Dale went east to work the Duray. I went with Pa to take their lunch.

MAY 15, 1967—Betty worked here on Sunday.

MAY 16, 1967—We got Donna's graduation announcement. We gave her $15 for a present.

MAY 17, 1967—The big tree (box-elder) is beginning to leaf out. It is very pretty.

MAY 19, 1967—The trees are getting green. It may freeze tonight and perhaps spoil the leaves.

MAY 21, 1967—June and Jane are getting confirmed today. We aren't going. They will work. Neil isn't feeling well or Pa either.

MAY 25, 1967—I went home with Betty to be there so that I could go to Donna's graduation. Betty brought me back the next morning.

MAY 29, 1967—Donna's boy friend gave her a lovely wrist watch for a graduation present. She also wears his class ring.

JUNE 9, 1967—Pa and I went to the hospital in Warren to see Oscar Bjorgaard today. He is quite poorly.

JUNE 10, 1967—We got a new washing machine lately. It is a Maytag and looks nice and works well too.
**It stood in the corner of the kitchen.*

JUNE 12, 1967—Uncle Jerry phoned Orrin yesterday that he and Eri would come up here on July 6th and stay until the 10th.

June 13, 1967—At Dairy Days in Thief River Falls, Donna got championship of all breeds. She gets the opportunity to travel to Waterloo, Iowa, for the Dairy Cattle Congress in the fall. June and Jane had blue ribbons. Arne had reserve championship.

June 14, 1967—Lanes were here from Brandon, (Canada), for dinner. They bought three cows for $600 apiece and $100 for delivery.
**The monetary value of each of these cows is about double the value of an average animal with no registration papers or butterfat production records.*

June 18, 1967—The boys are raking and baling hay.

June 24, 1967—We heard from Nancy. She thinks she can't come to see Uncle Jerry. They would have to come and go the same day.

July 2, 1967—We will have peas to eat before long.
**The first peas from the garden were targeted for the 4th of July. It was a major event for a farm family.*

July 3, 1967—We went to Radium on Saturday night and picked up the butter that the milk truck left there.
**The milk truck drivers usually carried both butter and cheese as a service for their patrons.*

July 4, 1967—A nice day. We all worked. We had new (garden) peas to eat and fried chicken for dinner.
**This menu was a favorite 4th of July treat.*

July 10, 1967—Uncle Jerry and Eri left for home today. Orrin, Neil and I took them to Grand Forks to fly back to Chicago.

July 15, 1967—Richard Tangen came to see Jerry. He left on Sunday.

July 18, 1967—We went to Barney Hanson's and looked at the berries, garden and flowers. They water the garden flowers with water from the river.

July 20, 1967—It is Nancy's and Arne's birthdays. We had a letter from Nancy yesterday. Granddaughter Ruth will ride in the Waterama parade. She is a little princess contestant.

July 25, 1967—I heard from Nancy regarding the plans for our (50th) wedding anniversary. She says the 27th of August is good for her.
**I needed to go back home and be ready to begin teaching at Villard the next week. This is when I taught in a house that was used as the kindergarten classroom. The house was later used as a private dwelling; however, at that time it had no separate rooms. I had thirty-three pupils in the afternoon so I could be a teaching assistant in the morning.*

July 27, 1967—Pa went to Thief River Falls and bought a brown suit today.

July 28, 1967—We've been given permission by Hagen to use the Alma Lutheran Church for the anniversary party.

**My parents were members of the Methodist church at Warren. The reasoning was that they wanted their 50th anniversary at a site that was centrally located for those attending from the neighborhood.

July 29, 1967—We went to Lawrence Hagen's to see about the ladies aid serving lunch for our 50th anniversary.

August 5, 1967—We went to Doris Anderson's to see about the wedding anniversary cake. She will make it and it will cost $25.

August 6, 1967—Neil and Jerry got Anna Thorson to cut the cake and Laverne Thorson so sing for our anniversary.

August 9, 1967—Neil had a heart attack; Jerry took him to the hospital. We will see him tonight.

August 10, 1967—Betty brought Pa's suit and invitations. Neil came home from the hospital. He feels quite well. They are combining like mad.

August 15, 1967—I have to freeze peas.

August 16, 1967—Elmer Johnson was here tonight. He has to go to the State Fair and demonstrate so can't be the emcee at our anniversary.

August 17, 1967—Pa and I saw about the napkins and notices in the newspaper and the "Thank You's" yesterday.

August 20, 1967—Pa asked the Methodist Reverend and his wife out for dinner next Sunday and then to be at the Alma Lutheran Church for our 50th wedding anniversary.

August 25, 1967—I went to Ione's and had my hair set.

August 27, 1967—Nancy and family came on Saturday for the anniversary. She is not feeling well and had a bad cold.

August 29, 1967—We had our Golden Wedding Anniversary on Sunday at the Alma Lutheran Church. There was a big crowd…about one hundred six signed the guest book. All of the grandchildren were in the program. Betty wrote our history in verse. Nancy described the timeless quality of a fifty-year marriage. There were many people from a distance. It was a lovely day.

**The following poetry reflects some thoughts on their special day.

> "Love's not Time's fool, though rosy lips and cheeks
> Within his bending sickle's compass come;
> Love alters not with his brief hours and weeks,
> But bears it out even to the edge of doom."
>
> —William Shakespeare

Ruth and Orrin

I should say of their years all fifty.
They did a job neat and nifty,
And of this precept, they did fully keep.
'As ye sow—so shall ye reap.'

—Betty Kruger Rantanen

SEPTEMBER 4, 1967—We labored on Labor Day. We did the laundry.
**Carrying all the water both in and out was heavy labor. The only running water was in the bathroom.

SEPTEMBER 9, 1967—We received no more anniversary cards so I guess that the anniversary is over.
**How touching is this? Mother savored their 50th anniversary celebration as long as she could make it last.

SEPTEMBER 22, 1967—I went to Edna Brosdahl's this afternoon and had lunch. We had a good visit.

SEPTEMBER 25, 1967—It froze last night. The corn is hurt.

OCTOBER 4, 1967—Jerry brought home a big bunch of bittersweet.
**We all loved the parasite with the bright orange berries that is a harbinger of the season.

OCTOBER 5, 1967—Donna works at the turkey plant in Thief River Falls. Betty had twenty goose hunters Saturday for the opening of the season.

OCTOBER 6, 1967—I made apple pie today. I also washed and set my hair.
**When I lived at home, Mother—as a matter of course—wore her long thick hair in a cornet of braids on her head. As she grew older, she could not tolerate the hairpins that were required for this arrangement, so she had her hair cut.

OCTOBER 8, 1967—It rained so there are puddles and it is cloudy but not terribly cold. The leaves are gone off the big tree!

OCTOBER 9, 1967—Selma hurt her wrist…her arm is in a cast. She wants Orrin to take her to the doctor on Friday.

OCTOBER 14, 1967—They are drying sunflowers today. I went along to see them combined. They leave long stalks.

OCTOBER 16, 1967—The combine broke down doing the sunflowers.

OCTOBER 22, 1967—Pa and I sat outside on the lawn. The boys are putting bales of straw around the foundation of the house.
**The bales provided additional insulation and plugged up some of the cracks in the drafty old house.*

OCTOBER 24, 1967—They have finished the sunflowers but have the corn to do yet.
**The cows had to be milked both morning and night in addition to all of the planting and harvesting chores. The herd of Brown Swiss was not sold until May 1968.*

OCTOBER 26, 1967—A miserable day. Pa got sick at the barn but is better now.

NOVEMBER 4, 1967—Jerry went to Nancy and Jim's on Friday evening to pheasant hunt. He took russet potatoes for them and Erickson's.

NOVEMBER 15, 1967—I went to the clinic today and got a flu shot and also had my blood pressure taken. It was 138 so is satisfactory according to Dr. Pummela.

NOVEMBER 17, 1967—Jerry went to Fargo to a roaring twenties party. He took Pa's old blue suit to wear (as a costume).

NOVEMBER 18, 1967—Neil and Orrin took Selma to the Dr. She got her cast off yesterday.

NOVEMBER 23, 1967—We went to Betty's for Thanksgiving and took Carl (the D.H.I.A. tester) along. They had a lovely dinner. Hjalmer (Betty's significant other) and Uno Rantanen (Betty's brother-in-law) were there. Hjalmer furnished the turkey and made a pie. I took cranberries and jell-o.

NOVEMBER 26, 1967—Neil's birthday. I had a turkey for dinner. Neil watches the football games.

My World Is Falling Asleep

My world is falling asleep.
Coating of white the winter will keep.
My world gray and depressed,
Laying its head for a winter of rest.
My winter white and serene,
Covered with snow, virgin, pristine.

My world is falling asleep.
Flowers in bud the winter will keep
My world lovely and fair,
Is all aglitter with crystals so rare.
My world is falling asleep
Coating of white the winter will keep.

—Nancy Kruger Olson
(Written Thanksgiving, November 1978)

December (?), 1967—We had a very elegant lunch at the Homemaker's party. I got an apron, lotion, two washcloths, candles and an ironing board cover.
**Such inexpensive gifts, but they were functional and clearly appreciated.*

December 11, 1967—It is snowing. I washed and ironed clothes. I looked at the Carol Burnett Show. It was funny.

December 14, 1967—It was a nice day. I baked Christmas cookies and frosted them.
**Mother traditionally made rolled sugar cookies and cut them into various shapes such as a camel, Santa, Christmas tree, angel, bell, or star. They were delicious and a labor of love.*

December 17, 1967—Betty brought an evergreen tree fresh cut from her property today. We got a poinsettia Nancy sent last night. It is very beautiful.
**I was teaching kindergarten at Villard and had the cash to spend for this plant, which I knew they'd appreciate.*

December 19, 1967—We got a card from uncle Jerry. This is very unusual for him.

December 20, 1967—IT'S A BLIZZARD!

December 21, 1967—The blizzard is subsiding but all of the schools are closed. We got the mail.
**Getting the mail was a major event after being cut off from the world by the swirling white powder. Sometimes the mail didn't come for many days and the only thing we'd have to connect us to the world was the radio. If you were to use the radio too much, the batteries would go dead.*

December 22, 1967—Jerry cleared the snow away. He went to town and got groceries.

December 24, 1967—It is snowing and blowing some. I don't know if we will all go to Betty's or not since the cows are expecting to calve.

December 29, 1967—They had to get the vet for the heifer to calve.

December 30, 1967—We heard from Nancy yesterday. They had a nice Christmas and were pleased with what we sent.

Coneflowers - 2008

Diary Entries—1968

January 30, 1968—The air reserves were called up for service because of the seizing of the Pueblo air craft carrier by (?). We heard from Nancy. They have fifty-one inches of snow. She had six days of school in January so far.

**Because I taught kindergarten—morning session and afternoon session—I missed more school. Either it started late or closed early because of all of the bad weather. I got so bored that I went over to school just to get out of the house, even though school hadn't opened. I had my own key, making it possible to get some planning done. We lived on a main road that usually was the first one to be plowed.

January 31, 1968—The Viet Nam War is not going good. The North Viet Cong are in Saigon. There is fighting around the United States Embassy.

February 5, 1968—I am reading "Nicholas and Alexandra." I like it quite well.
**I also enjoyed the story of the Romanov family, written by Robert K. Massie.

February 11, 1968—Jerry brought Ginny home from Fargo. He gave her an engagement ring...a diamond.

February 12, 1968—I don't know when Jerry and Ginny will be married. She wants to help her mother (with the resort) next summer.

February 13, 1968—Jerry had a letter from Uncle Jerry. He wants to know Ginny's name and where she lives.

February 16, 1968—Elling Jorgenson died last night at the hospital. The funeral is on Monday. It is a blizzard today...no school.

February 18, 1968—It is sunny and cold...-20. Elling Jorgenson's funeral is tomorrow. Orrin, Neil and Jerry are pallbearers.

FEBRUARY 19, 1968—Elling looked unnatural—too good.

**Mother is picking up on the funeral industry practice of dressing up and cosmetically enhancing the corpse to make it look better than life. Elling was a single man and was our next-door neighbor a few steps down the road to the north. We were there for each other. Elling allowed my dad to use his telephone when we had no phone, and he was traditionally invited to dinner on holidays.

MARCH 6, 1968—Altendorf (Hubert) will be buried in North Dakota on Friday.

**He was our neighbor to the south about a mile and one half. He had a housekeeper for a time, including her three children. They enrolled in our country school mid-term, causing quite a stir.

MARCH 9, 1968—Mary can get a loan (student) from the Middle River bank.

MARCH 10, 1968—Neil and I went to Thorson's to see LaVerne and Anna. Grandma Bjorgaard was fussy and we didn't stay long.

**Mother's use of the term "fussy" reminds me of my dad's phrase, "getting into his second childhood." It was a fortunate thing he never made it to that age.

MARCH 17, 1968—It is St. Patrick's Day today. I heard Irish music last night on the radio.

**Mother was quick to claim her Irish heritage bestowed by the Matthews who immigrated to America in the early 1700s.

MARCH 20, 1968—It is the first day of spring. There is lots of snow. There are many power lines down from the ice and wind.

MARCH 24, 1968—It is a nice sunny day—about 60 degrees above. Pa and I sat on the straw bales outside the house to sun ourselves.

MARCH 26, 1968—Mary has gone to the University.

MARCH 30, 1968—Orrin finished wall-papering the dining room. It looks very nice. I like it. It is pink paper.

MARCH 31, 1968—I talked to Nancy on the phone yesterday. Nancy wants Pa and I to come to her graduation from the University of Minnesota at Morris in June.

**They did not come. Neil was too busy with the haymaking, milking, and cultivating to leave and drive them.

APRIL 4, 1968—Orrin is painting the dining room woodwork white.

APRIL 6, 1968—Martin Luther King was shot last night near his motel. Everyone is excited over it.

APRIL 8, 1968—This is a day of mourning for Martin Luther King.

APRIL 9, 1968—It is King's funeral. It lasted about two and one half hours.

April 16, 1968—Ginny and her mother were here today. She was interviewed at Stephen today for teaching Home Economics.

April 19, 1968—Betty has been working here the past two days. Jerry and Betty have (been) working east.

April 30, 1968—Donna has an engagement ring from Armand Westlund. We had rhubarb and asparagus to eat from the garden.

May 4, 1968—Old Suzy had twin heifer calves.

May 8, 1968—Betty was here for breakfast. She wanted to start seeding the oats.

May 17, 1968—We went to see Edna Brosdahl today. She is alone.

May 22, 1968—I heard from Nancy. Alan will have his tonsils out.

May 26, 1968—The Hutterites from Fordville North Dakota were here and have made a deal to buy the cows. They paid down $2,000.

June 1, 1968—Jerry went to Ginny's graduation today. We sent roses.

June 3, 1968—Ginny and her mother, Delora Erickson, leave for Sweden and Denmark on June 10, and will be gone a month.

June 6, 1968—Bobby Kennedy was shot on June 5th at the Los Angeles victory celebration. He died this morning. An Arab shot (him) in the head.
**We were told of the shooting while we were at the Methodist Church teaching Vacation Bible School. Coming so soon after the death of Martin Luther King Jr. on April 4th, we were shocked and wondered who would be next. We were all sitting in church in stunned silence, and then Ellen Swanson led us in a prayer.*

June 7, 1968—Nancy graduates from the University of Minnesota at Morris tonight. We sent Nancy a travel set of three pieces. The Kennedy funeral is today. It is all we've heard for three days.

June 12, 1968—We got Donna's wedding invitation today. She will be married on June 29th at the Middle River country church.

June 14, 1968—Donna took Jerry's tea set for her wedding and wants Nancy to pour for her wedding.

June 18, 1968—I got a new dress. It is pink striped cotton…two-piece. I like it! I heard from Nancy. They will come for Donna's wedding. Jim has to go back the same day.
**There was no end to the farm work in the month of June with cultivating the corn, making hay, spraying weeds, and milking the cows two times a day.*

June 28, 1968—Betty was down today. She said that Armand broke his leg and will have to go on crutches down the aisle.

June 29, 1968—It was Donna's wedding day. It was a lovely wedding.

June 30, 1968—We all went to Yonkes to the Brown Swiss picnic. Jim and Nancy and family went along and left from there.

July 4, 1968—Neil, Pa and I went to see the Hutterite Colony at Fordville, North Dakota. It is very impressive with 20,000 chickens, 10,000 geese—looking very picturesque drinking in the river.

July 22, 1968—June got in the court of honor at the style review. Robert Barr was here on Saturday evening to sell his house to Jerry.

July 23, 1968—The Hutterites will get eight cows in the morning. Karl is here for the last time. **Karl was the Dairy Herd Improvement Association official milk tester. He provided the official butterfat production records that went with the cows when they were sold.*

July 26, 1968—They took the rest of the cattle today…all but three cows and the bulls.

July 27, 1968—Betty was here yesterday and paid her interest. Pa gave her the currents and gooseberries—also onions, peas and flowers.

July 28, 1968—Delaquis and friends stopped to look at the barn stanchions.

July 30, 1968—We heard from Nancy. They got a used piano for Ruth. **Ruth took piano lessons from various teachers, but music wasn't her niche. We realized many years later that Mark was the one who should have taken piano lessons.*

August 4, 1968—Neil took the last of the cows to Roy Johnson. **The Kruger's had a herd of registered Brown Swiss cows from 1930-1968. All things must come to an end. There would be no more Dairy Days, Brown Swiss picnics, county fairs, or state fairs, except through Betty's children who kept the faith picking up where Orrin, Neil and Jerry left off. Mother said nothing of their emotions or the gains and losses of the event. She merely reported it with her innate wisdom, staying safely in the moment. She looked neither forward nor backward on what had become a legacy of sorts. "Give your best, show to win, become the best you can be, and find ways to make the best even better."*

August 8, 1968—We had a letter from Nancy and a lovely picture of Lady Slippers. **We owned a marsh where the Lady Slippers grew. Actually, the pink Lady Slippers aren't supposed to be native to this area. We are too far south.*

August 16-17, 1968—Nancy and Jim came on Thursday afternoon and left this morning. Betty, Arne, Mary and Donna came down to see Nancy and Jim. We all had lunch. Nancy brought blueberry pie—also sweet corn and apples.

August 28, 1968—Hubert H. Humphrey got nominated to run for president on the Democratic ticket. The convention was a riot. I really mean it. (This was at the Democratic Convention in Chicago). The National Guard was there to quell the demonstrators. The police came into the convention hall.

**Our son Alan has written a book using the Democratic Convention of 1968 as a background for his science fiction. It is called Pure Existentialism.

September 6, 1968—We went to the Dr. today and got my blood tested for the teeth pulling. Everything is fine—both my heart and blood pressure.

September 12, 1968—I went along with Orrin to take lunch out. It was a beautiful day. Willie went along. They combined Selma's mustard yesterday.

September 17, 1968—I went to the dentist and had two molars out. I am very sore.

September 23-24, 1968—Ginny's mother, Mrs. Delora Erickson, has a lovely home on a hill with a beautiful lake view. We saw Ginny's stainless steel tableware. It is very odd looking.

September 25, 1968—Neil and Pa and I went to grandma Bjorgaard's funeral. Pa was a pallbearer. Grandma Bjorgaard was ninety-three.

September 26, 1968—Jane was here and got apples. She had her new class ring. She said Donna is pregnant and will expect in May of 1969. (This baby was Nathan).

October 18, 1968—Neil had two light heart spells today.

October 24, 1968—Pa and I went to Selma's and took her some beets. She gave us four big squash. She seemed quite well.

October 26, 1968—The boys are working like mad on the sunflowers.

October 28, 1968—The grain dryer caught fire when Neil was gone.

November 7, 1968—I went to Homemakers at Gerda Moe's. It was a dark, dreary day. We made Christmas ornaments.

November 12, 1968—I had five teeth and two bones taken out at Fargo.

November 13, 1968—My jaw is swelled a lot and black and blue. Also my throat has been very sore. They finished combining today.

November 15, 1968—Jerry is bulldozing trees with the bobcat.

NOVEMBER 16, 1968—We got four lovely colored pictures of Nancy and Jim and the kids at Lake Itasca and the logging camp at Park Rapids.
**We could only take short vacations and this was one of them.*

NOVEMBER 18, 1968—Orrin heard from Virgil Knaup (Orrin's cousin) today. He sold all of his cattle and machinery. He said Orrin should visit them as they are (both) getting up in years.

NOVEMBER 20, 1968—I went to the dentist and got my stitches out.

NOVEMBER 22, 1968—Orrin bought a lot of groceries for Sunday—turkey with trimmings. He also bought stocking caps for Mark and Alan.

DECEMBER 1, 1968—I wrapped up two Christmas gifts. My jaw still hurts.

DECEMBER 10, 1968—Betty was here this afternoon to bring the Christmas tree. I baked Christmas cookies today.

DECEMBER 11, 1968—I went to the dentist and found out I have an infected chin. It is very sore.

DECEMBER 12, 1968—We set up the tree today. It looks lovely.

DECEMBER 17, 1968—I fell over a rug and hurt my lip. My hand and arm are both black and blue.

DECEMBER 18, 1968—My chin is better.

DECEMBER 20, 1968—The men folks are incorporating the farming operation.

DECEMBER 27, 1968—Neil got sick in Grand Forks yesterday. Jerry took him to the clinic.

DECEMBER 31, 1968—Neil went to the Grand Forks Clinic. Jerry took him.

Sunflowers - 2008

DIARY ENTRIES 1969

JANUARY 2, 1969—Neil is in Grand Forks at the clinic again.

JANUARY 4, 1969—Jerry worked at the beet plant Friday night. He didn't like it and wouldn't go back again on Saturday!

JANUARY 8, 1969—I was at the dentist today. He took an impression of my mouth.

JANUARY 15, 1969—We went to town to sign the papers to incorporate the farm.

JANUARY 17, 1969—Mrs. Erickson is in the hospital with a heart attack. Jerry took Ginny Erickson home to Battle Lake.

JANUARY 19, 1969—Jerry got back from Erickson's. Mrs. Erickson is in the hospital at Fergus Falls and will stay two weeks.

JANUARY 20, 1969—We listened to the inauguration of Richard Nixon and the parade.

JANUARY 23, 1969—It is a very bad blizzard. There is no school today. We rummaged through the big trunk upstairs to find Orrin's Navy suit for Betty to wear at Middle River.

JANUARY 24, 1969—In the trunk I found an old letter from my dad—the last one he wrote in 1943— also, his marriage license to Luella Greg (his second wife). There were also some baby clothes.

JANUARY 31, 1969—The cows that the Hutterites got from us and their other cows were burned to death in a barn fire on Wednesday night. The fire was caused by a propane explosion.

FEBRUARY 1, 1969—The Hutterites saved ten cows. We don't know if they were some of our cows or not.

FEBRUARY 6, 1969—The boys (Neil and Jerry) went to see the Hutterites yesterday and found out that four of the cows that were not killed had been from our herd.
**This tragedy was humbling and fraught with emotion for the entire Kruger family.*

FEBRUARY 12, 1969—I went to the Dr. about my leg. I got new pills for my edema.

FEBRUARY 19, 1969—I wrote to Myrtle Tuffs Connor (Mother's first cousin), and gave her some family history that Nancy got from Springfield, Tennessee.
**Mother and I worked on the Matthews' family history before I left home. Later in life, I was able to complete it up to the Revolutionary War and far beyond—becoming a member of the Daughters of the American Revolution.*

FEBRUARY 25, 1969—The clothes (that we washed) and dried on the line—Pa took them outside. It has been thawing today and yesterday. Neil and Jerry went to Bathgate, North Dakota, to get an anhydrous tank.

FEBRUARY 28, 1969—I went to the dentist and will get my teeth next Thursday.

MARCH 19, 1969—I got my teeth today. They fit quite well. I can eat soft food with them.

MARCH 25, 1969—Selma was here. The boys bought her land. They took her to the lawyer.

MARCH 26, 1969—We heard from Nancy. Mr. Olson is very sick. They called everyone home.

MARCH 27, 1969—Betty was here last night and brought the eggs she made to give to Nancy's children. The eggs are unique and pretty.
**They were Ukrainian Easter eggs. We had them for many years.*

MARCH 28, 1969—Jerry leaves in the morning for Erickson's to practice on Saturday night for the wedding on Sunday.

MARCH 30, 1969—We stayed at Erickson's after the wedding and had a lovely supper and place to sleep. Betty and June were along with us.

APRIL 1, 1969—There were twelve attendants at the wedding. The bridesmaids wore green. They carried greens rather than flowers. The men wore tuxes.

APRIL 2, 1969—Ginny and Jerry went to Hawaii on their honeymoon. They will be back next Tuesday, flying into Fargo. They made a lovely couple.

APRIL 9, 1969—I heard from Nancy. Mr. Olson had a set back.

APRIL 16, 1969—Nancy phoned on Monday evening the 14th to say that Mr. (Morten) Olson died yesterday at noon. The funeral is Thursday. We may go.

April 17, 1969—We went to Mr. Olson's funeral at Glenwood. The children were all home.

April 18, 1969—It was lovely weather for the funeral and to come home today.

April 24, 1969—They are getting ready to go in the fields. The big tree is budding out. The grass is green.
**What a pretty picture Mother paints with the most economy of means.*

April 25, 1969—Orrin picked fresh rhubarb and sent it home with Jerry.
**My dad was frugal and didn't want anything to go to waste. It gave him much pleasure knowing Ginny would use it to make a tasty rhubarb cobbler or pie.*

April 27, 1969—Pa, Neil and I went to church and to Jerry's and Ginny's for dinner. We had a good meal: chicken and trimmings…a jell-o dessert with berries. The apartment looks nice and the wedding gifts are most unusual.

May (?) 1969—Betty went home with June. Neil paid her $100 for the nine days of field work.
**Betty needed the money to pay her property taxes.*

May 10, 1969—Betty phoned yesterday. Donna had her baby boy.
**This would be Nathan Westlund.*

May 11, 1969—Neil took Orrin to the hospital in Grand Forks yesterday. He has prostate trouble and has to have an operation.

May 13, 1969—Ginny took me to Grand Forks last night to see Orrin at the hospital. He was not too bad off, but had some discomfort.

May 14, 1969—The hospital phoned that Orrin had a fever (about 107) so I got Ginny to take me there. He felt better by the time we left (the fever had broken).

May 19, 1969—Neil took Jerry and me to Grand Forks to see Pa. He seemed cheerful but his mouth was sore. He will have his operation on Tuesday.

May 20, 1969—Orrin came out of his operation…it turned out well. He talks rational, but his mouth is very sore.

May 21, 1969—June and Jane got back to school again after being suspended.

May 23, 1969—Ginny took me to see Orrin today. He was despondent and said he has to have his operation, yet also has to take insulin (for diabetes).

May 25, 1969—Jerry and Ginny planted the gardens and mowed the grass in the yard while we were gone to Grand Forks.

MAY 27, 1969—We took Orrin tulips on Tuesday when we visited him.

MAY 30, 1969—Neil, Jerry and I went to Middle River to June and Jane's graduation and went to Betty's for lunch.

JUNE 1, 1969—Neil and I saw Pa today. He seemed stronger and walked alone.

JUNE 7, 1969—I went to Homemaker's at Klopp's today. We had election of officers, which produced hard feelings.

JUNE 8, 1969—We went to Grand Forks to see Orrin. He was feeling quite well and wants to come home for Father's Day.

JUNE 9, 1969—Uncle Jerry phoned today. He asked about Orrin's health. He said he was going to Brookhaven (National Laboratory) on Long Island, New York.
**Uncle Jerry was a nuclear physicist and was taking a sabbatical to do research. As a professor, he taught classes and conducted research at the University of Illinois at Urbana, Illinois.*

JUNE 12, 1969—Orrin just called and said that he will be coming home tomorrow.

JUNE 13, 1969—Orrin came home today. He is quite feeble, but better than I expected.
**My dad was hospitalized from May 11 to June 14. He nearly died of the high fever before they did the surgery.*

JUNE 15, 1969—Nancy, Jim and family came. It was a nice day.

JUNE 16, 1969—Betty, Mary, her boyfriend (Lou), Jerry, Ginny, and Armand; Donna, and baby Nathan came for Father's Day.
**This is when I took the four-generations photograph—Great-Grandmother, Ruth Emma Matthews Kruger; Grandmother, Elizabeth Kruger Rantanen; Mother, Donna Rantanen Westlund; and baby, Nathan Westlund.*

JULY 5, 1969—Ginny and Jerry looked at the Stanghelle place yesterday. She likes the house and grounds.

JULY 7, 1969—June was in a car accident on the 4th of July night near Argyle. She has a torn tendon in her arm…also cuts and bruises.

JULY 16, 1969—June is home from the hospital and looks like a patchwork quilt.
**The astronauts walked on the moon for the first time on my birthday, July 20.*

JULY 24, 1969—The astronauts got back from the moon and got recovered from the space capsule.

JULY 27, 1969—We went to Eunice and Lloyd's 25th wedding anniversary at Argyle. Neil spoke about Eunice and Lloyd as his schoolmates at the Schey School District #18.

AUGUST 8, 1969—Nancy writes that her brother-in-law (Dale Olson) is at basic training at Ft. Bragg, North Carolina.

AUGUST 15, 1969—Orrin and I fixed sweet corn and froze it.
**Sweet corn is considered the ultimate treat of the summer.*

AUGUST 17, 1969—Pa and I went to church. We heard the new minister speak. He doesn't wear a robe and is a young man.

AUGUST 28, 1969—Orrin picked a bucket of cranberries.
**Oh, how tasty are the wild, high-bush cranberries. They are a true gourmet delight.*

SEPTEMBER 30, 1969—We had one of the best visits we ever had with Nancy, Jim and Mark, Ruth and Alan.
**Considering Mother seldom made judgments about anything, this entry seems exceptional to me and of course makes me (as her daughter) feel happy all these years hence.*

OCTOBER 4, 1969—Orrin picked about one pint of raspberries.

OCTOBER 16, 1969—Neil took Selma to a lawyer to have her will made. Willie wants to go to the retirement home in Warren for the winter.

OCTOBER 20, 1969—Neil took us to Argusville, North Dakota on Sunday. We had good visit and trip. Corrine Hickey is a Tuff's more than a Kruger.
**Corrine was my mother's double cousin—her parents being Tuffs and Kruger.*

NOVEMBER 3, 1969—We washed clothes. They dried good outside.
**This no doubt was my dad's frugal side coming out, since they had a clothes dryer.*

NOVEMBER 12, 1969—Jerry took Orrin to the Grand Forks hospital. He was hemorrhaging again. He is in a ward with five men.

NOVEMBER 14, 1969—Neil took me to Grand Forks to see Orrin. He had his operation and was sitting up in a chair today.

NOVEMBER 15, 1969—Neil got sick at the hospital. I thought I wouldn't be able to get home but we made it.

NOVEMBER 17, 1969—Neil had a spell last night. I got Jim Nichols to come and stay awhile. I couldn't reach Jerry. Neil got better.

NOVEMBER 18, 1969—Neil didn't have to stay at the hospital as I had thought.

NOVEMBER 19, 1969—Orrin may be home by the end of the week.

November 21, 1969—Orrin came home from the hospital yesterday. He was not too bad off. He was quite cheerful.

November 1969—Uncle Jerry called from Upton, New York (where he is on sabbatical at the Brookhaven National Laboratory) regarding Orrin's surgery.

December 1, 1969—Jim and Nancy sent fish and venison with Jerry when he stopped there on his way home from Sauk Centre.

December 18, 1969—The television caught fire. There was a loose connection. Neil carried it out of the house and put out the fire.

December 23, 1969—We got a new television today. The old one caught on fire and got spoiled.

December 24, 1969—The Christmas Carolers were here last night. It was -16 below. Jerry and Ginny have gone to her Mother's at Battle Lake.

Nancy Powers – wedding portrait.
She married Jacob Matthews on October 17, 1844, in Jo Davies County, Illinois.

Jacob Matthews – wedding portrait, October 17, 1844.
Grandfather of Ruth Matthews.

19 73 Ella Henry & Duan
Byrgoind were here Sun
eve. Duane is workin
here for awhile

19 73 Pa & I found an
Grand ma's old paper
rack in Grandma's
old trunk up stairs.
We took it down &
hung it in the living
room. It looks remark
-ably nice. Even Henry
that it lovely. The
old trunk had a feath
bed in it on top of the
paper rack

19 76. It looks like it coul
rain. They are workin
on the living room (

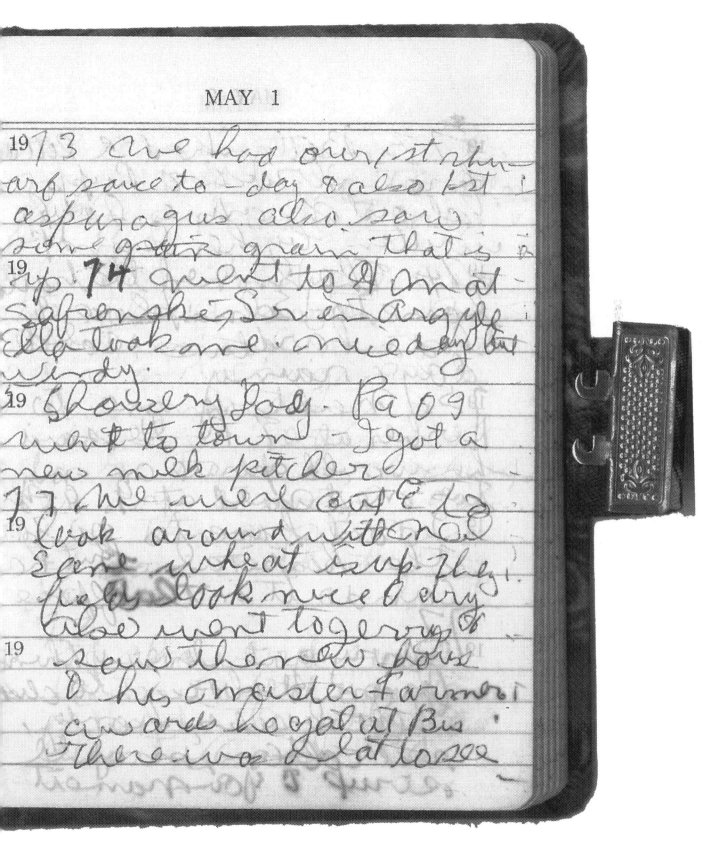

MAY 1

19/3 We had our *1st rhubarb sauce to-day & also 1st
asparagus. Also saw
some green grain that is up

19 74 went to 21 on at
Spring[?] Sev in Argyle
all took one nice day but
windy.

19 Showery day. Pa & g
went to town. I got a
new milk pitcher.

19 7 We were out & to
look around with no.
Some wheat is up. They
all look nice & dry.
Also went together
saw the new house
his master farmer
in are ho gal at Bus
There in a gl at to see

Two pages from Ruth's Diaries mid 1970s.

Ruth Matthews' Sunday School classmates and their parents circa 1911.
Adelia is the first person in the back row and Ruth is the first person in the second row.
Adelia and James Tuffs acted as Ruth's parents from 1903-1911. Their home was at Deer Creek, Minnesota.

Ruth Matthews' parents,
Edward Matthews and Emma (Immerfals) Matthews.
Wedding portrait circa 1894.

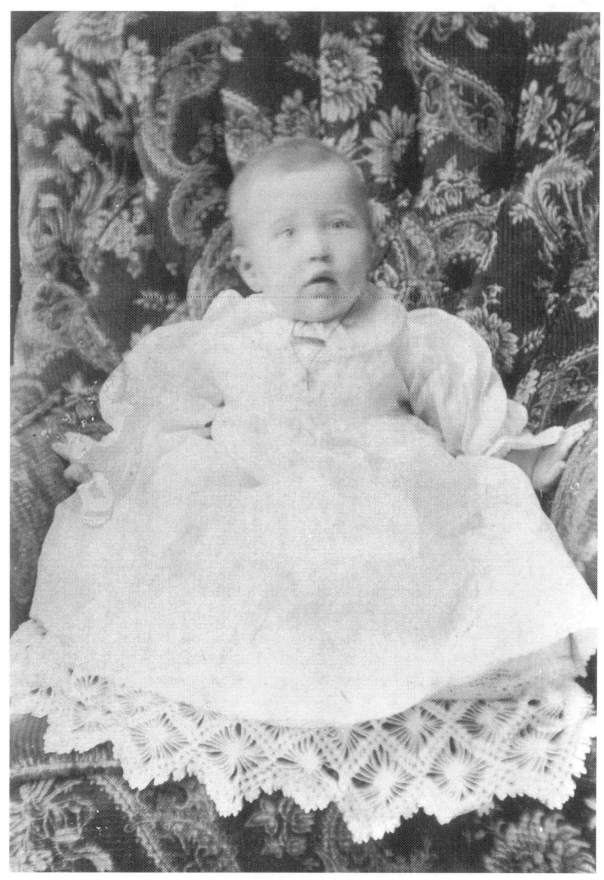

Ruth Matthews – baby portrait circa 1898.

My clothes of young days.

The first good dress I
remember was one, blue
trimmed in ... — blue braid
... I came to Aunt ...
in the spring & that
it very lovely but Aunt
Deal said it is spring
and you have to have
a white dress to go to S.S.
So Grandma made a fancy
white one lace, tucks & all.
Then she made 2 frilly
petticoats & a camisole of white
embroidery with slits for
a ribbon to be drawn
thru & bows.

My socks were either
white, pink or light blue &
patent leather slippers.
A big trunk of ...

"My Clothes of Young Days" by Ruth Matthews Kruger.

Ruth Matthews circa 1905 in her good dress — the white one to wear to Sunday School.

Ruth Matthews circa 1912, daughter of Ed and Emma Matthews.

Ruth Matthews circa 1911 with her parents, Ed and Luella Gregg Matthews.

Post graduate.

PUBLIC SCHOOLS
WADENA, MINNESOTA

REPORT

Of *Ruth Mathews*

Normal ~~Grade~~

For Year *1916 – '17*

STUDIES	FIRST SEMESTER						SECOND SEMESTER					
	1	2	3	Av.	Ex.	Av.	4	5	6	Av.	Ex.	Av.
Reading	85	83		84	88	85						
Arithmetic	82	82		82	83	82						
Language							75	84			92	84
Geography	79	85		82	89	84						
History							88	92			91	91
Spelling	85			85	86	85						
Writing				91	78		90				90	90
Physiology							85				75	80
Music							87	77				86
Dom. Science					80			88				84
Hf. Days Ab.	4	2					7	3	2			
Pedagogy	85	82		83	82	82	85	86			91	88
Drawing	81	81			81	81	82					83
Handwork	82	82			82	83	84					83
Agri.	91						90				93	92

Nelle Patchin

Teacher.

Ruth Mat(t)hews - Post graduate report card from Wadena Normal
(teacher's training) 1916 – 1917.

Wadena normal (teacher training) class of 1916 – 1917.
Ruth Matthews front row first on the left.
Class teacher, Nellie Patchin, second row in the center.
Ruth Matthews taught in the Minnesota rural schools from 1917 – 1919,
one of them near Frazee, Minnesota.

Kruger family circa 1943.
Back row: Betty Kruger, Neil Kruger.
Front row: Jerry Kruger, Ruth Kruger, Nancy Kruger, Orrin Kruger.

Wedding portrait of Ruth Matthews Kruger and Orrin Cornelius Kruger, September 1, 1917.

Winner of a free trip to the National Dairy Congress in Waterloo, Ia., this fall, which goes to the purebred champion, was 15-year-old Jerry Kruger of Warren, who showed a Brown Swiss. This was his third year of competition at the Thief River Falls event.

In the showmanship contest which ended the judging activities, Miss Nelda Mattson of Fertile took the honors with her poise and knowhow which neared professional stature. In previous years she has won second and third places in the showmanship contest, but this year, her sixth, she finally reached the top.

Taking second was Sheldon Erickson of Badger, while L a r r y Krezl of Angus, last year's showmanship winner, placed third. All three were commended by the judges for their skills.

An outstanding Holstein calf from the Paul Pierson farm in Washington County was awarded during the afternoon to Synneva Roragen of Fertile, who had last year's grade champion.

Winners in the various breeds were:

Holstein—Lois Erickson, Badger.

Milking Shorthorn — J e r o l d LaVoi, Fosston.

Guernsey — Bernard N e l s o n, Clearbrook.

Brown Swiss — Jerry Kruger, Warren.

Jersey — Marvin Peterson, Lockhart.

Ayrshire — Kathryn Dziengel, Kennedy.

The Northwest Dairy Day, largest regional event of its kind in the nation, was originated to build up and hold the interest of young people in the dairy industry. Guiding light in its founding and growth was Lew Conlon, who serves as manager of the Minnesota Dairy Industry Committee in St. Paul.

Jerry Kruger with champion Brown Swiss cow.

Circa 1956

...come to our services.

Two Brown Swiss Bulls Sold from Kreuger Herd

Two registered Brown Swiss bulls from the herd of Orrin C. Kruger and Sons of rural Warren have recently been sold to Brown Swiss breeders in other parts of the state, according to a report from Fred S. Idtse, secretary of the Brown Swiss Cattle Breeders association in Beloit, Wis.

Orrin Kruger sold the bull Dragnet Cleo's Apex, 134523 to Eugene Roger Paulsrud of Halstad and Jerry P. Kruger sold the bull Dragnet Dell's Corporal, 134699, to Norbert P. Fiedler of Little Fork.

Kruger Cow Produces 424 Pounds Butterfat in Test

Nellie's Daisy Lass 252922, a registered Brown Swiss cow owned by Orrin C. Kruger of Warren, has recently completed lactation records on herd test, 2x milking, according to Fred S. Idtse, secretary of the Brown Swiss Cattle Breeders association of Beloit, Wis. In 286 days the animal produced 10,989.7 pounds of milk averaging 3.86 per cent butterfat or a total of 423.91 pounds of fat.

75 Attend Canton 7 Picnic Sunday On Kruger Farm

About 75 persons attended the Brown Swiss Canton 7 picnic held at the O. C. Kruger farm Sunday. A short program was given on the rural Warren farm following a picnic dinner.

Included in the program was a musical selection by Carol Johnson of the West Prairie 4H club; demonstration by Mary Kay Larson of the West Prairie 4H club; talk on breeding, feeding and management by Harold M. Johnson, vocational agriculture instructor at Warren high school, and comments by Neil Kruger.

In his comments, Mr. Kruger pointed out that in 25 years of breeding Brown Swiss cattle the Kruger family had noticed an immense growth in the popularity of the breed in the area. The family has kept records privately and through the Dairy Herd Improvement association.

Mr. Kruger added that a 15-year-old Brown Swiss cow in the Kruger herd had produced 102,-394 pounds of milk and 4,228 pounds of buterfat. The remainder of the day was spent socially by those in attendance.

KRUGER SELLS BULLS

Orrin C. Kruger, Warren farmer and Brown Swiss breeder, recently sold the bull, Carmen's Northern Star, to Karl M. Holm of Tyler, according to Fred S. Idtse, secretary of the Brown Swiss Cattle Breeders association of Beloit, Wis. The Krugers have also sold the bull, Dragnet Nellie's Repeater, to Arne Rantanen of Middle River.

HARLEM'S CHATTER

Well, I'm back from the State Fair now, but still have a few things to tell you.

To me the busiest building at the fair was the cattle barns on Saturday, August 31, when all the 4-H livestock was being judged.

Some of the 4-H'ers were down at the barns at 5 a. m. because they had to be ready to show by 8:30 a. m. Judging continued all day until 6:30 p. m. when the Dairy Showmanship contest was held. Sylvia Sorter participated in it.

At 7:30 p. m. the annual 4-H Livestock Show was held. All blue ribbon animals were paraded before the public in the Hippodrome. Incidently, that Hippodrom eis a tremendous building. It has no supports inside, so where ever one sits, your vision is clear. It is in this building that all the judging was done.

Also that evening awards were given to the Grand Champion winners and the showmanship winners.

* * * *

Jerry Kruger was interviewed by Maynard Speece on WCCO radio on Monday, September 2, on his 12 noon Farm broadcast. As you know, Jerry was the Grand Champion Brown Swiss exhibitor.

* * * *

Minnesota has 5,900 4-H club members in the diary project. They are learning better selection, feeding and management of animals.

Also, there are 3,500 4-H members in the beef project in our state. They, too, are learning better selection, feeding, and management.

* * * *

Terry Dahl was elected Honor Camper at Farm Boys Camp by members of his squad. This gives him the honor to go back next year to the camp as an Honor Captain.

* * * *

Junior Livestock Show is coming soon. The dates are September 30-October 3 at South St. Paul.

We just received a new bulletin in the office. It is entitled "Here's your 1957-1958 Minnesota 4-H Program." It is prepared and written by your State 4-H offices. Why not stop by and get one?

* * * *

Many of the 4-H clubs have elected new officers already. Some haven't. Keep in mind that your officers will be running your club for the coming year. They should be good responsible willing work-

Orrin and Ruth Kruger taken on Easter Sunday circa 1948 by their daughter Nancy.
This photograph was later used as a resource to do the wood block print featured in this book.
Ruth wears dress up clothing, her best coat with the hem of her fancy apron protruding. Orrin wears his denim
jacket and overalls.

Ruth and Orrin Kruger circa 1960.
This was taken before she had her hair cut. She wore it in a braid on top of her head. It was secured by hair pins
which eventually grew too painful, leading to her choice to have it cut short.
They are standing by Orrin's pear tree. It was his pride and joy and survived until killed by −60 temperatures.

Ruth Kruger's grandchildren circa 1964.
Ruth, Alan and Mark Olson.

Ruth and Orrin Kruger's wedding anniversary celebration
at Alma Lutheran Church on August 28, 1967.

Ruth's grandson, Mark Olson, seated in "The Big Tree" at the Kruger farmyard.

This photograph reveals the effects of the blizzard on March 2-4, 1966.
It was taken looking south from the door of the farmhouse. Jerry Kruger took this iconic image.

Orrin seated on the riding mower next to his tulip bed 1966. It went from snow in March to tulips in May.

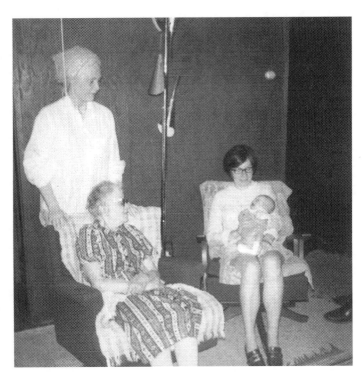

Four generations of Ruth's family 1969.
Standing: Betty Kruger Rantanen
Seated: Ruth Matthews Kruger, Donna Rantanen Westlund with infant son, Nathan Westlund.

March 30, 1969, at Amor, Minnesota.
Virginia Erickson's wedding to Jerry Kruger.
Delora Erickson, Virginia Erickson Kruger, Jerry Kruger, Ruth Kruger, Orrin Kruger.

Ruth's grandchildren with daughter, Betty Rantanen, center front row circa 1975.
Back row: Jane Hirst, Arne Rantanen, Donna Westlund.
Front row: June Troskey, Betty Rantanen, and Mary Efta.

Jim Olson family portrait circa 1973-1974.
Back row: Jim Olson, Alan Olson, and Mark Olson.
Front row: Ruth Olson holding Hattie, and Nancy Kruger Olson.
Photograph by Dale Olson.

Three generations of Kruger men.
Jerry, Garth, and Orrin circa 1975.

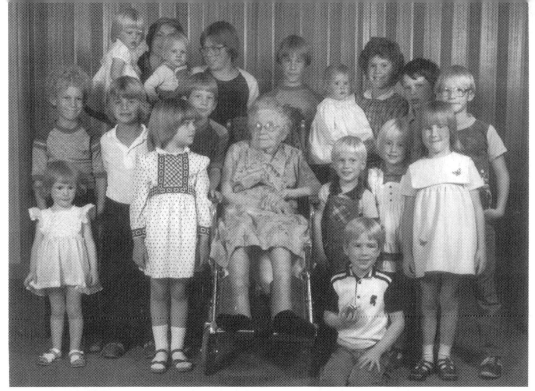

Ruth Matthews Kruger with grandchildren and great-grandchildren circa 1981 at Good Samaritan.
Back row: Meredith Kruger held by Mother, Ginny Kruger, Amber Efta, Nathan Westlund, Paul Troskey, Nicolette
Westlund held by sister Heather, Garth Kruger and Tony Troskey.
Middle row: Jacob Efta, Ivan Hirst, Joseph Efta, Ruth Matthews Kruger, Jed Efta, Tasha Hirst, and Jennifer Troskey.
Front row: Lacey Hirst, Muria Kruger, and Joshua Efta.

Ruth with grandchildren – Christmas 1981.
Back row: Alan Olson, Ruth Olson, Mark Olson, Donna Westlund, Jane Hirst, Mary Efta, June Troskey.
Front row: Meredith Kruger, Garth Kruger, Ruth Kruger, Muria Kruger.
Photograph taken at the home of Jerry and Ginny Kruger.

Ruth Matthews Kruger with son, Neil Kruger, circa 1986.

Kaisa Efta circa 1979-1980.
Ruth Matthews Kruger's great-granddaughter.
Daughter of Lou and Mary Efta.

Alex Efta circa 1979-1980.
Ruth Matthews Kruger's great-grandson.
Son of Lou and Mary Efta.

Melissa and Anne Rantanen III circa 1980.
Great-grandchildren of Ruth and Orrin Kruger.
Children of Arne and Diane Rantanen.

Ruth Kruger with her great-grandchildren, Lacey and Waylon Hirst, circa 1983.
Children of Jon and Jane Hirst.

Ruth Kruger's great-grandchildren, Lily and Logan McLaughlin, 2007.
Their parents are Craig and Ruth O. McLaughlin.

Neil and Nell Cheney Horgan Kruger.
They were married May 23, 1991, at the Warren Methodist Church.

Ruth Kruger's Christmas 1985 with her granddaughters, Muria and Meredith Kruger.

Ruth with family friend, Joyce Elvehjem, circa 1986 in the Good Samaritan.

Books I Read in Lower grades 1-4
The Lonesomest Doll
Little Colonel
Alice in Wonderland
Robinson Crusoe
Toby Tyler, 10 yrs with a circus
Five Little Peppers
Stepping Heavenward.
grade 4 to 8
Little Women
Jo's Boys
Little Men
Alger Books
Elsie Dinsmore
Black Beauty
Beautiful Joe
Great Stone Face
King of the Golden River
Random reading by teachers
Peck's Bad Boy
The ...
Uncle Tom's Cabin

"Books I Read" – Ruth Matthews Kruger.

Ruth Kruger's 90th birthday at the Good Samaritan Home, Warren, Minnesota.
It was celebrated at Christmas of 1986 rather than her actual birthday on February 13.

Lady's Slipper - 2007

Diary Entries--1970

January 3, 1970—Orrin was to Grand Forks with Neil. He has blood poisoning in his arm and has to keep a moist hot pack on it.

January 26, 1970—The sno-cat races are on now. They start at Winnipeg and go to the Twin Cities. Twenty-four contestants started the race.

February 1, 1970—It changed from 28 above this morning to ten below this evening. It is a bad blizzard—the worst yet this winter.

February 6, 1970—I heard from Nancy. They are getting a new colored television. It is an RCA Portable.
**It was our first color television.

February 23, 1970—It sounds like June might get married.

February 24, 1970—Ginny says June has an engagement ring. Bob Barr wants Jerry to buy eighty acres of his place and the house.

February 25, 1970—Nancy sent a picture of the children on their red snow sleds. Mark had on the red mitts we gave him for Christmas.
**The sleds were called "mini-boggins" and were made of red plastic.

March 19, 1970—Nancy writes that Dale's wedding is at Glenwood on Palm Sunday at the Methodist church.
**He was getting married to Janet Musselman Zody from Indiana.

MARCH 23, 1970—The mail strike is still on…we get no letters but we got the Grand Forks Herald.

*This is inconsistent—we didn't get the newspaper. Jim happened to get one from a friend who lived in town, and he read it over and over as if he couldn't get enough of it.

MARCH 26, 1970—We went to town to the lawyer's office. We signed the papers for Neil to buy the farm. We get to live in the house (as long as we wish).

MARCH 30, 1970—June will be married on April 25, 1970 in the Catholic Church at Middle River. Her fiance's name is Clayton Troskey. He is nice looking…tall and dark—nineteen years old.

MARCH 31, 1970—Betty had to help a sheep have a lamb.

*This is something I have not done. Betty loved her animals and would have made a fine veterinarian. It was something where having small hands and experience counted. Maybe the lamb came breech; maybe something was tangled up inside the ewe; maybe the lamb was a big male and was hung up on her narrow hipbones. Betty knew all of these possibilities and much more.

APRIL 4, 1970—I heard Sister Thomas More speak at the P.K.M. (electrical cooperative of Polk, Kittenson, Marshall, Counties) in Warren. She spoke on the different farm organizations amalgamating.

APRIL 7, 1970—Orrin gave Betty $25 to help on June's Wedding.

APRIL 14, 1970—I heard from Nancy. They won't come for the wedding. Jim has to work. They will come in June.

*Jim was planting and milking cows and I was teaching in Starbuck.

APRIL 17, 1970—The astronauts got back safely to earth. We saw them splash down. They couldn't go to the moon because of trouble with the space-craft.

APRIL 26, 1970—We were to June and Clayton's wedding at Middle River. There were lots of gifts and the drinks flowed freely. There were three men (groomsmen). June looked lovely. Mary and Jane were bridesmaids.

MAY 9, 1970—Kent State Shootings. The University of Minnesota students were rioting (and the campuses were shut down) all over (the state) on account of the (United States) troops going into Cambodia. Six students were shot. Four of them died, and others were injured. They were shot by National Guardsmen at (Kent State University) in Ohio.

*I was taking an off-campus class at Benson from Dr. Ray Lammers at the University of Minnesota at Morris. The class was cancelled for at least one session, since the entire university system was shut down in an effort to avoid any more bloodshed. There is no describing the visceral feeling in the pit of the stomach after seeing college students being shot and killed by National Guardsmen on a college campus in America. Recently I've been told that it was one of the pivotal points in initiating the end of the war in Viet Nam.

MAY 12, 1970—We had a good fried chicken dinner.
**Oh, for the days of fried chicken gone—alas, like our youth too soon.*

MAY 14, 1970—I heard from Nancy. She has lost 17 pounds on diet pills.
**Thanks to Dr. Bucher and his prescription. I learned absolutely nothing about food, lower calories, recipes or that exercise was a necessity.*

MAY 18, 1970—The crocus are in bloom. The big tree is very fairy-like with its light green tinge.
**Mother and Dad worshipped the big box-elder that grew in the front yard. My dad said that fairies lived there.*

MAY 19, 1970—Orrin worked in the garden. We have lots of asparagus.

MAY 20, 1970—It is still wet so the boys are getting stuck a lot. There is some grain up. The tulips have buds.
**This reminds me of a song we sang in kindergarten:*

Spring

The air is warm
The sky is blue
The leaves are green-yellow,
Because they are new.
The feet go skipping.
The birds all sing.
The whole world is happy
Because it is SPRING!

MAY 26, 1970—Nancy called last night. They have direct dialing now. She was happy about it.

MAY 3, 1970—I saw a baby moose at Blavik's yesterday. It weighed about fifteen pounds.

JULY 1, 1970—Roger Cole got his induction notice for July 23rd. He can't get deferred. It is a new law.

JULY 2, 1970—Neil doesn't feel well. He is worried about finding another hired man.

JULY 22, 1970—June will go to Texas since Clayton (Troskey) has gone there for his (basic) training.

AUGUST 1, 1970—(Chet) Huntley (of the broadcasting team of Huntley and Brinkley) had his last day of broadcasting last night.

AUGUST 8, 1970—Orrin and I looked at the sunflowers. They are in blossom and are very beautiful.

AUGUST 9, 1970—It is smoky and dry. We could use rain. Orrin is still picking raspberries.

AUGUST 12, 1970—Louie Launderville from near Stephen is working here. Betty picked a box of chokecherries and stayed for supper.
**Chokecherry juice mixed with a few raspberries and some lemon juice makes a superb jelly.*

AUGUST 15, 1970—It is cool and cloudy with light rain. I fixed one pint of gooseberries to freeze and one pint of currents.

SEPTEMBER 2, 1970—Our 53rd wedding anniversary. June and Clayton came to see us. They came from Texas. He has two weeks of vacation, which included six days of traveling.

SEPTEMBER 6, 1970—Ella and Henry Bjorgaard were here last evening. Ella brought pictures of the French children Darlene adopted. They are cute.

SEPTEMBER 22, 1970—Jim's uncle's funeral (John Morton) was a big affair according to Nancy. There was weeping, laughing, hugging and kissing.

SEPTEMBER 24, 1970—The leaves are beautiful now.
**I wrote this (poem) as a young girl upon seeing the aspen trees glowing in the afternoon sun.*

Golden Torches

Golden torches line the sky.
Row on row...high on high.
In their brightness
How they shine.
Have you seen the
Trees in autumn Time?

—Nancy A. Kruger (1949)

NOVEMBER 4, 1970—Bob Berglund got elected over Odin Langen...Hubert Humphrey for senator and Wendell Anderson for Governor. Many Democrats got elected.

DECEMBER 2, 1970—Pa and Neil and Jerry bought $10,000 of those debentures in California. I was MAD.
**Perhaps my mother had not been consulted about this rather large investment.*

DECEMBER 16, 1970—Betty brought us a big picture she painted. It is of scenery with a Brown Swiss cow and a new-born calf with Mary by their side.

DECEMBER 26, 1970—Betty, Arne and Jane were here for Christmas. It was a nice day.

DECEMBER 29, 1970—Sabol brought back the $10,000.
**The debentures were no longer available or sold out.*

Diary Entries 1971

JANUARY 2, 1971—We had watermelon from out garden to eat. I can't have Homemakers…my leg is too painful.

JANUARY 5, 1971—I went to Dr. Lamb about my arthritis. He gave me some extra medication.

JANUARY 6, 1971—Orrin had a long session at the clinic. He has to take insulin.
*This is a telling note. My dad loved his Christmas treats—especially the sweets. He lost a lot of weight and went on to manage his diabetes with great care.

JANUARY 18, 1971—Ginny made Pa a (flannel) nightshirt for his birthday. He was pleased.
*My dad was six feet tall. Commercial nightshirts—the ones they ordered from the catalog—were never long enough.

FEBRUARY 1, 1971—The water froze up yesterday. Neil and Jerry are working on it.

FEBRUARY 18, 1971—Arne got $200 worth of conservation awards according to an article in the Warren Sheaf.

FEBRUARY 19, 1971—The boys are working on Jerry's barn. They are tearing out the cement—getting it ready for use as a place to store grain.

MARCH 14, 1971—Jerry, Ginny, Neil and I went to Donna's for the baby's baptism. It was a misty-cloudy day. It is very wet under-foot. Armand's folks were there. We had a good lunch.
*This baby was Heather.

MARCH 18, 1971—The boys went to Canada after gypsum. There were several trucks that went.
*Sometimes gypsum is used on acidic soil to correct the problem.

MARCH 26, 1971—Orrin got a letter from Eri. Uncle Jerry had a stroke and can't move either his right arm or leg.

MARCH 27, 1971—Neil called Eri. She says Uncle Jerry is getting along quite well.

APRIL 7, 1971—I had Homemakers. It was a lovely day. Ginny helped some with the serving.

APRIL 14, 1971—Eri called last night. I talked to her. Uncle Jerry is in a nursing home.

APRIL 22, 1971—Orrin planted potatoes in the garden today.

APRIL 27, 1971—The boys started in the field yesterday.

MAY 2, 1971—Orrin and I took off the storm windows and cleaned the windows. It was a lovely day.

MAY 3, 1971—Jerry had an accident. He broke a wheel off the tractor.

MAY 5, 1971—I heard from Nancy. Jim's cousin, Jack Morton's wife (Charlotte Torgeson Morton and their daughter), were killed in an automobile accident near Tintah.

MAY 14, 1971—Nancy called. She will teach half days next fall.

JUNE 6, 1971—We all went to Arne's graduation at Middle River. It was a lovely warm day.

JUNE 19, 1971—Pa picked three pints of strawberries from our patch.

JUNE 20, 1971—Richard Tangen, wife and two children were here this afternoon. They went to Jerry's.

JUNE 22, 1971—Neil has had pneumonia and has been quite sick.

JULY 16, 1971—We had cherry pie from our own tree today. It was good.
**This was a proud day for my father. He enjoyed planting trees and bushes that he could nurse along, often raising plants that were not suited for northern Minnesota.*

JULY 20, 1971—Ginny picked the currents and June-berries at Edna's (Brosdahl's) place.

JULY 22, 1971—We had new sweet corm for dinner.

JULY 23, 1971—I made five glasses of current jelly from the currents that Ginny picked. I gave her two of the glasses.

JULY 28, 1971—Orrin called Eri on Sunday. There is no change in Uncle Jerry, going by what she says. He can walk with some assistance.

July 29, 1971—We got three snapshots from Nancy yesterday…one of Orrin with Heather at Jerry's place…one of Nancy with a big fish and one of Ruth.

August 14, 1971—Betty phoned last night. June had a 10 ½ (pound) baby boy.
**This was Paul Troskey.*

August 26, 1971—The state fair begins. Ruth Olson has a demonstration on baby-sitting (it was called Chester Manymesser and the Baby-sitter.) Ruth's cousin, Mary Rantanen, also went to the state fair as a dorm counselor.

August 28, 1971—Orrin picked a pail of cranberries.

September 2, 1971—Ruth got a blue (ribbon) on her babysitting demonstration. Nancy, Jim, Mark and Alan went to the fair on Friday.
**Ruth was twelve years of age—just old enough to go to the fair with a demonstration. She wore her hair in ponytails.*

September 11, 1971—I went east with Orrin. I had to wait about three hours for him. The truck caught fire. They had to put it out on the road.
**Grain dust is flammable and only needs a spark to ignite it.*

September 14, 1971—Nancy called to say there was a bomb scare at her school.
**The school was evacuated over noon hour. I was not informed and sat in my secluded kindergarten room waiting for the afternoon class to arrive. When the clock indicated the children were past due, I went upstairs to look for the bus that brought them or some word as to why they were so late. As I walked down the eerily quiet halls, I discovered that I was the only person left in the building. One look out the front door told the story. All of the busses had picked up the kids and the area was cordoned off. I grabbed my purse and ran out the front door, leaving my classroom behind.*

September 29, 1971—I heard from Nancy. She gets to have a full day of teaching.
**I had been scheduled for half time in the spring. When fall came, I had thirty or more children, so I was given a contract to teach full time.*

October 1, 1971—Pa and I picked six pints of raspberries.

October 3, 1971—The boys found out on Saturday the gypsum deal was a gyp—to the tune of $1,250.

October 14, 1971—Orrin and I planted (tulip) bulbs.

October 19, 1971—Orrin and I made carrots for freezing.

October 30, 1971—Betty was here and said Jane was getting married on December 18, if her fiancé is able. He was in an accident (Kenny Felling). Jane's intended was in a drag race accident and has a brain concussion.

NOVEMBER 8, 1971—Betty phoned today and wants Ginny and Jerry to be host and hostess at Jane's wedding on the 18ᵗʰ of December.

NOVEMBER 17, 1971—Jerry says Arne will be married soon.

NOVEMBER 18, 1971—Jerry got a nice fawn while hunting at Nancy's.

NOVEMBER 21, 1971—We went to town and bought Arne and Jane wedding gifts.

NOVEMBER 25, 1971—This is Thanksgiving and we are alone…that is; Neil, Pa, and I. Arne will be married tomorrow evening. Jerry is the best man.

NOVEMBER 29, 1971—We went to Arne's and Diane's wedding. Jerry was the best man and June was bridesmaid. Diane's brother and wife were also in the wedding. The reception was at a hall near Thief River Falls. Betty was wearing a wig.

DECEMBER 1, 1971—I went to Selma's birthday party. I had a good lunch and time.

DECEMBER 20, 1971—We went to Jane's wedding in December at Brooks. It was a Catholic wedding.

DECEMBER 24, 1971—Betty brought a (fresh cut) tree on December 22. We set it up on the 23ʳᵈ. Jerry and Ginny went to Erickson's. I have a bad cold and also Neil.

DECEMBER 24, 1971—We were alone for Christmas; Pa, Neil and I. Neil watches the football games.

Diary Entries 1972

January 2, 1972—Mary (Rantanen) has an engagement ring from Lou Efta.

January 24, 1971—There was a bad blizzard. Neil went in the ditch coming from Birger's. He stopped at Bagaas's and walked home from there.

March 20, 1972--Diane (Arne's wife) is expecting soon.

March 31, 1972—Betty wants Neil to take her to Minneapolis on Sunday evening. She will be on television Monday at 6:30 A.M. She will be speaking about soil conservation.

April 7, 1972—Betty had her picture in the Warren Sheaf with a write up about her winning the conservation award at the state of Minnesota.

April 9, 1972—Orrin bought ten Warren Sheaf's with the story about Betty winning the award. We sent them to relatives and friends.

April 12, 1972—I have a terrible upset stomach.

April 20, 1971—We went to town and bought Mary and Lou a pressure cooker for a wedding gift.

April 22, 1972—Pa heard from Uncle Jerry today. He wrote a nice letter with the help of the therapist. He and Eri walk ten blocks a day.

April 28, 1972—Orrin started to plant garden: Potatoes, corn, lettuce and radishes.

May 1, 1972—Betty has hurt her fingers. She came and got our milker so she didn't have to milk by hand.

MAY 16, 1972—George Wallace, the governor of Alabama, was shot yesterday. He is still alive.

MAY 19, 1972—Orrin is mowing the lawn for the first time (this season).

MAY 20, 1972—George Wallace's legs will be paralyzed. He'll campaign from his hospital bed—using television.

MAY 29, 1972—Nancy, Jim and Ruth came up for Mary's wedding at Terrebonne. It was Catholic and old style.

JUNE 13, 1972—We got a birth announcement from Diane and Arne. They have a baby girl, 5 pounds and eleven ounces.
**This was Melissa Rantanen.*

JULY 1, 1972—Orrin got a letter from Uncle Jerry. He does well writing with his left hand.

JULY 28, 1972—We saw a sand-hill crane in the garden this morning. He must have slept there, as he got up and walked around for awhile, and then flew off to the east. He was quite a sight—long legs and neck.

JULY 30, 1972—Richard Tangen was here from Hawley. He has a beard for the 100th anniversary of Hawley. I am busy freezing peas, string beans and raspberries.
**My mother is seventy-five years old by this time and functioning as a much younger person.*

AUGUST 15, 1972—Orrin heard from Eri. Uncle Jerry is about the same. He may have to go into a nursing home.

AUGUST 16, 1972—Eri called and wanted to come to the Grand Forks air terminal with Uncle Jerry's visit; then, fly directly back. Orrin said "No."

AUGUST 19, 1972—A very dry day—good for combining. It was 96 above in the shade.

AUGUST 24, 1972—Mary was here with Diane's baby (Melissa). She is expecting a baby in October.

AUGUST 30, 1972—Neil had chest pains. He went to the doctor. He sent him to the hospital.

SEPTEMBER 2, 1972—Neil was in the hospital at Warren. He came home on Saturday and (is) somewhat better.

SEPTEMBER 8, 1972—Neil, Pa and I put down the new carpet in the bedroom. It was hard work. The carpet is brown and gold and very nice and soft. I like it!! Neil went to Dr. Pumela for his check-up. He was O.K.

Wheat - 2008

SEPTEMBER 14, 1972—Eri phoned that it is alright for Pa and Neil to be at their place next Wednesday, the 20th. I will go along and stop at Nancy's until they come back on Thursday evening. We will leave on Sunday, the 17th.
I was teaching kindergarten at Starbuck at the time and virtually remember nothing about this trip.

SEPTEMBER 17, 1972—Pa and Neil left for Uncle Jerry's place. They stopped at Virgil's at Beaver Dam over night. Then they went on to Uncle Jerry's on Tuesday morning to arrive late Tuesday afternoon. On Wednesday, they visited with Uncle Jerry. They ate lunch and supper and then left about 7 P.M. On Thursday, September 22nd, Pa and Neil were again at Virgil (Knaup's).
Virgil was a nephew of our grandmother, Minnie Knaup Kruger, and my dad's cousin. They grew up together at Beaver Dam when my grandparents lived there for a short time—about 1905-1906.

SEPTEMBER 24, 1972—We got back from Nancy's and Jim's about noon. We had a good trip.

SEPTEMBER 25, 1972—Neil and Jerry went into the wild rice business, investing $15,000 with Sabol.

SEPTEMBER 27, 1972—When I was at Nancy's I saw the Pope County Museum and went with Mrs. Helen Olson to a coffee party at Sedan. There were thirty-five people there at 10 A.M.

OCTOBER 2, 1972—We went to see the wild rice paddies near Red Lake—also, the lake—and went through the reservation. Jerry drove. Ginny went along. It was a beautiful trip.

OCTOBER 12, 1972—We went to Newfolden with Anna to see the rolling pin factory and bought a lefsa rolling pin for Ginny.

OCTOBER 29, 1972—Betty phoned to tell us Mary had her baby boy on the 24th at Red Lake Falls (This was Joseph Efta).

NOVEMBER 8, 1972—Neil went to the Dr. in Grand Forks for a check up. The doctor said that Neil was in good health except he should lose twenty pounds and be careful of becoming diabetic.

NOVEMBER 17, 1972—Neil had a heart attack. Jerry took him to the hospital.

NOVEMBER 18, 1972—Neil has oxygen and a heart monitor.

NOVEMBER 24, 1972—Betty was here for dinner. We went to see Neil. He was sitting up in a chair today.

NOVEMBER 25, 1972—Neil had a set-back, so had the heart monitor again. It was very stormy.

NOVEMBER 29, 1972—We went to see Neil. He still has the heart monitor but talked quite a bit; but is discouraged.

DECEMBER 8, 1972—Neil got home from the hospital today.
*Neil stated that none of these episodes were heart attacks. It was a combination of stress-induced hypoglycemia and diet.

DECEMBER 11, 1972—Betty and June brought the Christmas tree.
*Betty always cut a fresh evergreen for my parents. They were especially aromatic and Mother enjoyed them so.

DECEMBER 11, 1972—Jerry had to take Neil back to the hospital.

DECEMBER 13, 1972—We saw Neil at the hospital. He looked quite chipper.

DECEMBER 15, 1972—Neil was depressed. He wants to go to the Mayo Clinic at Rochester or the University hospital.

DECEMBER 18, 1972—Neil came home from the hospital for overnight. He seemed quite cheerful and walked quite well but was weak.

DECEMBER 19, 1972—Jerry took Neil to Rochester to St. Mary's Hospital. He was supposed to fly but the weather was unsafe for flight. Jerry and Ginny got back from Rochester at noon.

DECEMBER 23, 1972—Neil got home from the hospital. Mrs. Olson (Helen) got him from Rochester and took him to Nancy and Jim's house. Jerry got him from there. At the clinic they advised him that he had nerve trouble. Nancy sent back fish and fruit.

DIARY ENTRIES 1973

JANUARY 16, 1973—It is Orrin's birthday. He is seventy-eight years old. Ginny brought him an angel food cake and fruit.
**Now that he is aware of diabetes, his diet has to reflect it.*

JANUARY 25, 1973—Former president Lyndon Johnson died of a heart attack.

JANUARY 25, 1973—The Viet Nam peace treaty is signed. We are happy the war is at an end after 11 or 12 years (of death and destruction).

FEBRUARY 8, 1973—Orrin and I went to town. I got this diary for a birthday gift.

FEBRUARY 13, 1973—I went to Homemakers. They gave me a birthday party. They had a big cake, cards, a scarf, handkerchief and tray. Eleven members were there and it was stormy.

FEBRUARY 22, 1973—We went to see Selma at the hospital yesterday. She said she was going to sell her (household goods) this summer or fall.

FEBRUARY 23, 1973—I got my new spring cotton dress. It is pink flowered and very nice!
**Such enthusiasm! And I'm guessing it was ordered sight unseen from the Montgomery Wards catalog.*

MARCH 19, 1973—It was a rainy and snowy day. We washed clothes and hung them out…so they were nice and wet!
**I'm thinking to myself…yes, I know who had the idea to hang them out (my father) and who had to wring them out (my mother) and put them in the dryer to get dry.*

MARCH 29, 1973—Jane and Kenny were here today. He is going to work for the boys.

APRIL 3, 1973—Kenny began work (today).

APRIL 7, 1973—Two Mennonites from Winkler were here today and wanted to buy the windmill to take to South America. They are moving to Bolivia.

APRIL 23, 1973—We went to Donna's for Easter. She had a good dinner and lunch. It had snowed on Saturday so we had a white Easter.

APRIL 29, 1973—Kenny quit working.

MAY 9, 1973—Nancy says they want Granny Olson to exchange houses with them. They need the bigger bedrooms since the kids are getting older.

MAY 13, 1973—We sent copies of the Civil War (letters) and the (1814) will from James Powers in Bath County Kentucky to Fern Kent Wilkenson.
**These letters and documents had been in the wooden box that Jacob, Edward and Ruth Matthews brought in the covered wagon when they traveled from Dubuque to Deer Creek in the late fall and early winter of 1903. The box was given to Ruth as a young child. The most significant letter was written by Richard and Agnes Matthews, who were living in Robertson County, Tennessee, at the time. The 1826 letter was sent to their daughter-in-law, Lucinda Snelling Matthews, in Bath County, Kentucky, in sympathy over the loss of her husband, William Matthews, who died from pneumonia. William Matthews was Jacob Matthews' father. Fern Kent Wilkenson was Adelia Matthews Tuffs' granddaughter and my mother's cousin.*

MAY 21, 1973—Orrin's apple and plum trees are blooming.

MAY 25, 1973—We stopped on the way back from Argyle and helped Neil fix his sunflower planter.

JUNE 6, 1973—I heard from Nancy. They had a tornado drop down near their place. It took two barns and a machine shed. Jim, Mark and Alan helped Terhaar's clean up the mess.

JUNE 17, 1973—Nancy, Jim, Ruth and Alan and all of Betty's children and grandchildren were at Jerry and Ginny's for Father's Day. Nancy brought FISH.
**Jim's prowess as a walleye fisherman is legendary.*

JUNE 21, 1973—I went to the clinic at Warren. I had blood pressure of 150 after being 190 (previously).

JULY 3, 1973—I fell and hurt myself yesterday. I cut my lip, nose and head. I was sewed up and let out of the hospital. Ginny got dinner today.
**My mother Ruth is seventy-six years old at this time. She is getting fragile and losing her sense of balance.*

JULY 12, 1973—Neil bought two (window) air conditioners…one for us and one for him. He and Jerry installed them this morning.

JULY 18, 1973—Mary, Lou and Joe were here on July 17th…Mary's birthday. Lou will work evenings and Saturdays for Jerry.

July 21, 1973—Ginny told us she is expecting a little newcomer around the 15th of December.
**This was Garth.*

July 23, 1973—It is the end of the Warren Fair. We didn't go. We went east to view the crops. They look good.
**Not going to the fair, was this perhaps the first time?*

July 28, 1973—I shelled about a quart of peas.

July 30, 1973—Jerry sold wheat for $3.15 a bushel at the Luna Elevator.

August 3, 1973—They are swathing and combining grain.

August 8, 1973—It is raining, and also rained last night. The men folks are so discouraged about combining. There is too much rain.

August 12, 1973—Ginny took us to June's to help Paul celebrate his second birthday.

August 14, 1973—Orrin picked cranberries…so I am knee deep in fixing jell(y) and jam.
**What a charming expression.*

August 15, 1973—They are still combining out east. Wheat is $5.06 (a bushel) now. It is the highest in our history of farming.

September 1, 1973—It was our wedding anniversary today. We are married fifty-six years. It was a rainy day. We stayed home.
**It comes to that. On our 51st wedding anniversary on December 22, 2007, it was cold and very windy. We stayed home. It was more blustery on the 23rd; but since we were invited to a friend's house, we ventured out even though the visibility was poor because of the drifting snow.*

September 9, 1973—We went to Nancy's. We got there about 7 p.m. We saw the kids get ready for Farmer's Market Day. They made $33 selling apples.

September 12, 1973—Orrin and I went to town to shop. He has a lot of insulin reactions lately… so doesn't feel well.

September 16, 1873—We had a heavy frost last night. It was 20 degrees. The heater gave out and also the water softener.

September 18, 1973—We went to Dr. Herber in Thief River Falls. He gave me a shot in the knee (cortisone) for arthritis. I got new arthritis pills.

September 19, 1973—Betty went to Warren to take the land out of the soil bank. She is renting 400 acres at $5 an acre.

SEPTEMBER 28, 1973—It is a lovely day. The leaves are yellow, red and russet. The big tree (box-elder) has almost shed her leaves.
*I can't help but notice that Mother has given the box-elder a gender. I learned this poem, "September," as a child and enjoy reciting it when September comes:

September

The golden rod is yellow,
The corn is turning brown,
The trees in the apple orchard
With fruit are bending down.
The gentians bluest fringes
Are curling in the sun.
While dusky pods of milkweed
Their hidden silk has spun.
All these lovely tokens
September days are here.
With autumn's best of weather
And season's best of cheer.

—Helen Hunt Jackson

SEPTEMBER 30, 1973—Ginny took Neil and I to the doctor in Thief River Falls. Neil's nerves gave out again. I went for my blood pressure test. It was 160. Lou helped Jerry combine. Lou and Ginny were here for dinner. Orrin made it. It was turkey and baked potatoes.

OCTOBER 10, 1973—Spiro Agnew resigned today.

OCTOBER 13, 1973—Pa, Neil, Jerry and I went to Langdon, North Dakota to look at a ten bottom plow. They decided to buy it.

OCTOBER 14, 1973—It was a lovely day to go to Langdon. We saw the missile base and the Turtle Mountains near Pembina.

OCTOBER 20, 1973—They are finished combining the sunflowers. Jerry is glad because he is sick and it has been hard on him.

OCTOBER 21, 1973—Ginny says Jerry has an abscess on his rectum. It is very sore. He can't work and is in bed.
** Sitting on an abscess while combining takes bull-headed determination.

OCTOBER 22, 1973—Neil took Jerry to Thief River Falls yesterday and he had his abscess lanced. We stopped to see him after visiting Selma at the nursing home.

OCTOBER 23, 1973—It is 72 above this morning. Orrin and I sat outdoors for a long time.
**Mother and Dad knew how to seize the day.

OCTOBER 31, 1973—Neil went to Thief River Falls to the Dr. He found out he has low blood sugar (hypoglycemia). Stress also played a role and diet.

NOVEMBER 4, 1973—Neil went to Nancy's today and then will go to Rochester tomorrow.

NOVEMBER 13, 1973—Neil came back from Rochester. He didn't find out anything (further), only what he knew from before.

NOVEMBER 22, 1973—This is Thanksgiving Day. It is nice (weather). Pa, Neil and I are alone (together). We had fish to eat.

NOVEMBER 26, 1973—We went to town to shop. (I) fell in the Coast to Coast store. (I) cut my head and bent my glasses but bought Jerry and Ginny's baby-to-be a present.

NOVEMBER 28, 1973—Ginny took Orrin to the hospital in Grand Forks today because of his hemorrhaging and diabetes.

DECEMBER 1, 1973—We went to see Orrin at the hospital. He can't come home until Tuesday or Wednesday.

DECEMBER 2, 1973—Orrin called. They are going to look at his bladder and prostate tomorrow. He seemed very emotional. I am sad.

DECEMBER 3, 1973—I got my new coat. We sent for it. It is dark brown and plush…very nice and not too heavy and it fits well.

DECEMBER 4, 1973—Orrin called last night. He didn't have to have the exploratory operation yesterday, but will today. He felt good.

DECEMBER 5, 1973—Orrin had his operation on Tuesday and was very miserable. It is the worst one he ever had. Betty's girls called when he was feeling the worst so he didn't feel like talking.

DECEMBER 6, 1973—The gas pipe-line broke and spilled 20,000 (gallons) of gas. Six tankers went past to try to save some of it. The spill is (only) five miles from here.

DECEMBER 9, 1973—Neil went to get Orrin home from the hospital. The power was off last night and again this afternoon. The storm has subsided but it is getting cold and the furnace has quit.

DECEMBER 11, 1973—Orrin feels somewhat better and not so nervous.

DECEMBER 15, 1973—Lou was here. He and the boys looked at places to rent or buy but found none. Neil got sick.

DECEMBER 17, 1973—Clayton called on Sunday evening the 16th and said that June had a baby boy. It weighed six pounds and they named it Anthony Clayton.

December 18, 1973—Ginny has been calling for Jerry. He finally got home and was going to take her to the hospital at Crookston for the baby's delivery.

December 19, 1973—Jerry and Ginny had their baby boy at 2 a.m. today. He is between six and seven pounds and is named Garth John.

December 20, 1973—Ginny and the baby are doing well. I went to help Ginny with the birth announcements.

December 21, 1973—Jerry gave us a snapshot of the baby…he and Ginny. The baby looks like him and weighs 8 pounds and 3 ounces and is 20 inches long.

December 23, 1973—Jerry and Ginny went to Mrs. Erickson's on Sunday. Muriel is there to help. Nancy called to say "Merry Christmas."

December 25, 1973—It was a nice mild day. Betty, Lou, Joe and Mary came for Christmas dinner. Mary brought jell-o salad and a picture of Joe. Betty brought about ten pounds of unsalted butter.

Christmas When I Was A Child

'Merry Christmas,' Mother called from the foot of the stair.
Glad tidings of joy filled the chilly dry air.
Stockings were hung at the foot of the bed,
Holding popcorn, oranges and an object of red.
We opened our gifts, a doll, book or toy.
But mostly remembered our feelings of joy.
Father was ebullient, robust and gay.
He'd purchased the candies for this winter's day.
The kitchen was spicy, pungent and cozy.
We welcomed our guests, cheeks colored rosy.
Elling our neighbor was never left out.
Joining our circle with nary a doubt.
And bowing our heads for grace to say,
'Lord love and protect us this blest Christmas day.'

—Nancy A. Olson (2007)

December 27, 1973—Grandpa Troskey died and was buried on Saturday. He was ninety-three or ninety-four.

December 30, 1973—June called. The baby (Anthony) is in the Grand Forks hospital and they will fly him to the University of Minnesota hospital on Saturday. A doctor accompanies the baby.

Ruth and Orrin - 2008

Diary Entries 1974

JANUARY 1, 1974—It is thirty-nine below this morning. We were alone but for Jerry. He came this afternoon.

JANUARY 2, 1974—Clayton and June went to the cities to see their baby. June will stay there awhile.

JANUARY 5, 1974—We took the tree down on the third. The needles were shedding (something) terrible.

JANUARY 7, 1974—Betty called to say that June, Clayton and Jane were coming home from the University Hospital and left the baby Tony. He had open(-)heart surgery.

JANUARY 9, 1974—June, Clayton and Paul were here today. They had been to Warren to seek assistance for the debt from the baby's surgery. He is getting along well.

JANUARY 13, 1974—It is cold and blizzardy. It never got to be above zero. It was thirty below yesterday. The hot water froze in the sink.

JANUARY 14, 1974—It took all day to thaw out the water. June's baby has to go back again to the hospital for a check up.

JANUARY 19, 1974—Mary and Lou and Joe were here. Lou rented Gustafson's land and bought a trailer house at Red Lake Falls...and will move it onto Elling Jorgenson's place.

JANUARY 30, 1974—Lou says that Mary is caring for June's baby so June can (get some) rest. The baby can't cry very loud.

JANUARY 31, 1974—Neil took Jerry to Crookston. He will have his operation tomorrow on his colon.

February 3, 1974—Neil, Ginny, Garth and I went to see Jerry at the Crookston Hospital. He seemed quite chipper and thought he could come home Tuesday.

February 5, 1974—Mary and Lou said that June was better and they had taken the baby home.

February 11, 1974—Donna, Armand, Heather and Nathan were here. They had been to the sno-cat races. Armand's sno-cat had (engine) trouble so he couldn't race. The kids are lively.

February 15, 1974—Duane Bjorgaard came over on Wednesday evening and brought me birthday cake and raspberry sauce…and stayed for lunch.

February 22, 1974—Neil took me to Grand Forks and I had five more x-rays…three for gall bladder and two for my chest. All were fine…no diabetes or sugar in the urine.

March 9, 1974—Neil, Orrin and I went to see June and Clayton and the kids. The baby, Anthony, is doing well. He weighs eleven pounds at three months.

March 15, 1974—This is a blizzard. School let out at 1:00 p.m. Mrs. Erickson, her sister, and daughter come tomorrow.

March 28, 1974—It is misting and very chilly.

April 16, 1974—Kenny Felling is at Glenwood to work on the railroad (Soo-line).

April 23, 1974—Jerry took Neil to the Doctor in Thief River Falls. He got different tranquilizers and is better.

April 25, 1974—June and Clayton, Tony and Paul were here in the afternoon. Clayton said that Kenny had an appendicitis operation on Saturday at Alexandria.

May 2, 1974—They moved Mary and Lou's trailer-house to Selma's place.

May 6, 1974—They began to seed at Selma's today. Pa and Mary worked in the garden.

May 16, 1974—Jerry took Neil to the hospital at 11 p.m. He had an overdose of pills.

May 19, 1974—Clayton Troskey graduates from the Tech-School at Thief River Falls.

May 22, 1974—Neil came home from the hospital yesterday. Ginny brought him home. Neil has to quit taking his tranquilizers and other pills.

June 17, 1974—We went to see Selma. Her sister and niece are here to help her get ready for her auction sale on the 29th of June. Selma walks with a cane.

June 24, 1974—Nancy, Jim and the kids came for Father's Day. Alan and Mark stayed at Betty's over night. Everyone went to Ginny's on Sunday.

July 7, 1974—We went to Mary and Lou's last night. Her great aunt and second cousin from Sweden were here…also Ollie and Lillian and Mabel Rantanen.

July 15, 1974—I hurt, or rather, cut my arm on the car seat belt when we went to Argyle for milk.

July 21, 1974—Nancy came on Thursday morning and left this morning at 5:30…She took Pa and I to the fair on Saturday morning for two hours.
**They seemed quite fragile and had difficulty walking, especially my mother; however, I was not accustomed to being around them on a regular basis. It is the only time that I took them to the fair.*

July 23, 1974—Saturday evening was Nancy's birthday party at Ginny's. She was forty. Mary and Lou were there. We had a good supper.
**I was so touched by the attention. I've never had a real sit-down birthday party in a private home. The effort did not go unnoticed and was much appreciated.*

July 24, 1974—Ginny's Mother died of a heart attack on the night of the 24th. The funeral is Monday the 29th at 10:30 a.m.

July 27, 1974—We all went to Selma's auction sale. Orrin bought a sugar and creamer for Nancy for $20. It is an antique.

August 2, 1974—Diane left Arne last Sunday and will live in Thief River Falls.

August 8, 1974—Nixon resigned and Gerald Ford took office at noon. Nixon resigning is the first in history.

August 9, 1974—We went to see Ethel Grochow yesterday afternoon. She came home from the hospital. We took her berries and cake.

August 13, 1974—Orrin picked the cranberries yesterday. He got about six quarts.

August 16, 1974—Betty got back in her house.
**Arne and Diane had been living in it. Betty lived in the hunter's housing, which was not insulated.*

August 19, 1974—The wheat is quite good but it has a lot of pigeon grass in it. It was under contract at $4.50 a bushel.

August 26, 1974—Carl Bjorgaard had a heart attack and Willie Wallin a stroke. He is ninety-five.

AUGUST 28, 1974—Willie Wallin died on the 26th. His funeral is tomorrow at the Baptist church. Neil is a pallbearer.

**I've never been asked to be a pallbearer. I suppose it isn't something I'd want to do and thus far haven't been asked. I did write a memorial reading for my friend Jenny's service at the United Parish Church.

SEPTEMBER 1, 1974—It is our wedding anniversary of fifty-seven years. We went to church and then to Donna and Armand's. It was a cool cloudy day.

SEPTEMBER 3, 1974—Orrin's watermelons are very good. They are nice and sweet.

SEPTEMBER 7, 1974—Nancy called to say they had a frost there that froze the corn.

**This was the first day of school.

SEPTEMBER 17, 1974—Betty was featured in the Midland Cooperator this week. It was a write up about her conservation (practices).

SEPTEMBER 30, 1974—The boys finished combining the mustard. It had blown around a lot.

OCTOBER 10, 1974—It was over seventy degrees above this afternoon. Pa and I went to town. The boys are combining sunflowers. I got myself a pants suit.

**This was my mother's first pants suit. Somewhere in this same time frame, I made myself a pants suit. I had to get permission from the superintendent of the Starbuck schools, Robert Boyd, before I could wear it while teaching my kindergarten class.

OCTOBER 28, 1974—It was over seventy degrees above this afternoon. Ginny, Garth and Jerry were here. We sat outside.

NOVEMBER 10, 1974—Mary took Orrin and I to vote. It was a nice day. The election went Democrat.

NOVEMBER 11, 1974—It was sunny with no wind. It was a lovely day. We sat on the bales (in front of the house) for awhile. Orrin went for a walk.

DECEMBER 10, 1974—I fell yesterday in the hallway by the stairs. I slipped on the rug. I got a bad black eye and a small cut above my eye from my glasses.

DECEMBER 11, 1974—I didn't go to the doctor about my eye. I put some ice on it and that helped a lot. I was in a hurry as Pa was going to Mary's (I wanted to go along). I was on the phone talking to Ella Bjorgaard (and somehow caught the corner of the rug).

DECEMBER 16, 1974—The (Christmas) tree is so lovely to see...so bright and gay. Neil put it up.

DECEMBER 19, 1974—Orrin and I went with Ginny to Mary's to celebrate Garth's birthday. We gave him blocks. Ginny brought rosettes and cookies.

DECEMBER 20, 1974—My face is getting better but it is still black and blue.

DECEMBER 24, 1974—We were to Jerry's and Ginny's for Christmas Eve supper. We had lefsa, lutefisk and plum pudding.

DECEMBER 25, 1974—We were to Lou and Mary's for Christmas dinner. Garth had fun with Joe's toys. He can walk but gets tangled up in his blanket.

DIARY ENTRIES 1975

JANUARY 1, 1975—I have Homemaker's Club at Anna's tomorrow. They will have a shower for Mary.
**This baby was Jacob Efta.*

JANUARY 11, 1975—It was a very bad blizzard. It was the worst in a long time. The temperature is fifteen below and no travel is advised.

JANUARY 16, 1975—It was Orrin's eightieth birthday. Jerry, Ginny and Garth came. Ginny brought an angel-food cake.

JANUARY 17, 1975—Lou called to say that Mary had a baby boy on Orrin's birthday. They named him Jacob Orrin.
**What a memorable birthday gift—a third Great-Grandson to carry the Kruger-Matthews-Efta-Rantanen genes.*

JANUARY 23, 1975—Neil, Pa and I went to Mary and Lou's to see the new baby. His name is Jacob Orrin. He is small and cute looking. Mary wants to get a job in welfare. She went to Oklee to be interviewed on Friday. Lou drove her there.

JANUARY 24, 1975—Jerry and Ginny went to help Charles (Erickson) move the furniture from her Mother's house. It is rented for $200 a month.

FEBRUARY 5, 1974—We were to Mary and Lou's house. They had Jacob Orrin baptized at the house and Mary joined the (Catholic) church in Argyle at the same time. Pat Efta and Jane (Felling) were sponsors. There were twenty-five or more at the house and two priests. It was a long baptism. Betty, June, Donna, Heather were there and also Jon Hirst that works at Betty's.

FEBRUARY 21, 1975—Jon Hirst took Betty, Jane, Lou, Mary and the kids to the Crookston winter shows.

FEBRUARY 24, 1975—Jon Hirst stays at Betty's and works as a railroad cook. He likes Jane.

FEBRUARY 28, 1975—Pa has an owl living in the Quonset building.
**Owls often seek shelter in barns and outbuildings during the cold winter months. It reminds me of the owl that we found one spring when I was in high school.*

MARCH 2, 1975—We were to Betty's. She was alone. Jane had gone fishing. She is expecting a baby in May or June. Kenny comes around once in awhile.

MARCH 11, 1975—It is a stormy day and the town board election. Neil was re-elected to the town board.

MARCH 24, 1975—This is a bad blizzardy day…with no travel advised.

MARCH 29, 1975—Neil and Henry Bjorgaard went to talk to Henry Schey about the early settlers in Alma Township (which were the Schey's). Neil is writing the Alma township history.
**This was to be printed in the Marshall County History Book.*

APRIL 25, 1975—Neil, Lou and Jerry cut down the trees by the garden to make room to build the new house. Jerry brought Garth here last night. I took care of him while they worked in the garden. He is not feeling well so was quite fussy.

APRIL 30, 1975—I found my Grandmother Matthews' old paper rack in Grandmother Kruger's old trunk upstairs. We brought it down and hung it up in the living room. It looked remarkably nice…Ginny thought it lovely too.
**It was a piece from the Victorian era that protruded from the wall in a sort of V-formation and was made to hold magazines or other paper objects.*

MAY 2, 1975—Neil took me to Dr. Herber at Thief River Falls. He said he would operate on my toes next Wednesday at 9 A.M. I don't have to go to the hospital. He can do it in the office.

MAY 5, 1975—Orrin picked a crocus today. The boys expect to start in the field.

MAY 8, 1975—Dr. Herber straightened my toes. He took out the crippled joints. That was yesterday. Today I can walk on my foot.

MAY 13, 1975—I went to Thief River Falls yesterday and had my foot dressed. It looks good.

MAY 16, 1975—Ginny took me to Thief River Falls to get my toe stitches out. There was some infection. I have to go back on May 27th to see about its progress and get one stitch out.

May 20, 1975—Orrin has planted a lot of garden by the machine shed. It needs to rain.
**Father's former garden had been taken over by Neil's new house.*

May 22, 1975—The chokecherry and plum blossoms are out and very pretty.
**Mother knew how to live in the moment.*

May 26, 1975—Pa's tulips are blooming nicely and his apple tree is a sight to behold.
**So much joy taken with the simplest of things.*

June 12, 1975—Jane had her baby boy at 12:30 a.m. She named him Ivan Kenneth. He weighed eight pounds. Jon took Jane to the hospital. Kenny (the Dad) called Mary with the news.

June 13, 1975—Jerry is digging the basement for the new house today.

June 14, 1975—Betty was here last night. She was quite upset about Jane, Kenny and the baby, Ivan.

July 2, 1975—There is a bad flood. Stephen, Warren and Argyle had about five inches of rain. The river is rising fast. We went to see it. It is over the road for some distance by Bagaas's. Laverne's pigs were up to their bellies in water. The fields are under water for fifteen miles. Lou and Jerry tried to put traps in the culverts to divert the water. The roads are going to pieces in many places. Nancy phoned. They had a bad hail storm. It destroyed most of their corn crop. They didn't have insurance on the corn—just beans.

July 4, 1975—Orrin and I looked at the flood going east. The electrical line poles are in the water in four places. They are Ottertail Power Company poles. At Argyle, Highway 75 was washed out so we had to turn around. It was a sad sight.

July 6, 1975—We looked at the crops. The water is going down but the grain looks sick.

July 15, 1975—Mrs. Helen Olson (Granny) just got back from a trip to Scotland. She traveled with her son Dale. It was a good trip. She visited six cousins at Boghead Farm.
**When we went to Scotland in 1995, two cousins, Robert and Jean Lambie, remained at the Boghead Farm. Neil and wife Nell went along and our daughter Ruth did the driving. Robert's voice had the same timbre as my husband Jim's.*

July 21, 1975—There has not been any work done on the new house for a month.

July 29, 1975—Jane and Kenny Felling are getting a divorce.

August 3, 1975—It is Sunday and a nice cool day. We rested. Pa picked berries. The boys tried to combine on Lou's but it was too wet.

August 4, 1975—The construction men are hauling sand for the basement of the house.

AUGUST 8, 1975—Mary brought over some green beans. Orrin bought a crate of peaches for $4.39.

AUGUST 12, 1975—Neil took me to Dr. Herber today to get care for my arthritis. I got a cortisone shot and some pills.

SEPTEMBER 4, 1975—The men came today to work on the new house.

SEPTEMBER 11, 1975—The construction men have been working all week on the new house and have most of the outside walls put up.

SEPTEMBER 15, 1975—Neil took us to Grand Forks to pick out wood and style of cabinets. We will have oak and light green Formica counter tops and thirty inch counter tops and thirty inch counters and lowered cupboards.
**This seemed like the thing to do at the time, since my mother was less than five feet tall. However, when Neil moved out and Garth and bride Richelle moved in, it was awkward for both Garth and Richelle, who are over six feet tall. Some renovations were necessary.*

SEPTEMBER 16, 1975—We called Nancy about Helen Olson. Nancy wrote that her Mother-in-law had a stroke. She wrote that her son Clyde took her to (Metropolitan Medical Center) in Minneapolis. She went by ambulance. She is in a coma. Jim found her about 11 A.M. on Sunday morning on the floor of the bathroom.

SEPTEMBER 18, 1975—Orrin withdrew $12,000 from the bank for the new house.

SEPTEMBER 20, 1975—The roof is on the house now. It is green.

SEPTEMBER 23, 1975—Nancy called this morning to tell us that Helen Olson passed away last night. The funeral is on Friday. She did not regain consciousness.
**This is when Granny Olson passed her final good-bye to me through the children's singing in my kindergarten class. They sang Twinkle Twinkle Little Star, which became a "Hallelujah choir" of intensity and brightness, and then the message came, "I'm alright—don't worry about me."*

SEPTEMBER 24, 1975—They are putting the windows in the house.

SEPTEMBER 27, 1975—We got back from Nancy's where we attended Helen Olson's funeral. The trees were in their most brilliant hues near Detroit Lakes. We saw all of the Olson boys and most of her eighteen grandchildren. We brought home tomatoes, apples, carrots and squash.

SEPTEMBER 28, 1975—The funeral was a large one with beautiful flowers. Nancy had us out for lunch instead of being at the church. We stayed in a lovely motel called the Hi-View. Jim paid for it. Nancy gave us breakfast and dinner. Ginny and Garth were at Nancy's for lunch and then left for Foster's at Sauk Centre.

OCTOBER 2, 1975—We had our last sweet corn. It was good.

OCTOBER 10, 1975—Orrin took in his carrots. It is the last of the garden. He also picked one pint of raspberries.

OCTOBER 15, 1975—Orrin finished putting paper around the base of the old house. I guess we'll be in it this winter as they haven't worked on it this week.
**One more winter in the drafty old house, and one more winter in the new house for my dad.*

OCTOBER 22, 1975—Jim and Nancy are going to rent the house Helen Olson lived in to a young couple.

OCTOBER 24, 1975—Neil took me to Dr. Lamb in Warren to get tested for glasses. I had the old ones for five years.

OCTOBER 26, 1975—My stomach bothers me a lot. The boys have been filling in the yard by the new house. Orrin took me to look at it. It was so hard and frozen on the ground I could scarcely walk and could barely get to the house.

OCTOBER 28, 1975—It is a cold cloudy day. We washed clothes and hung them outside.

NOVEMBER 3, 1975—It is a lovely day—about 60 above. We sat outside for awhile.
**What a charming portrait. Two elderly lovers—married fifty-eight years—as they sat sunning themselves on a warm November day.*

NOVEMBER 6, 1975—Orrin picked a few raspberries.

NOVEMBER 14, 1975—We picked out the carpet for the new house.

NOVEMBER 24, 1975—I was quite sick on my stomach today. I vomited a lot. Orrin washed the clothes.
**The arthritis medicine most likely was having an impact on her digestive system.*

DECEMBER 14, 1975—I baked Christmas cookies.

DECEMBER 17, 1975—The hot water in the kitchen is froze up.

DECEMBER 18, 1975—I made nut-bread yesterday. Pa and Neil went to town and took my glasses to be adjusted. The cabinets are here. The men have been staining and varnishing them.

DECEMBER 26, 1975—Nancy and Jim came and brought the dish cabinet.
**The storage unit had been made for Helen Olson's collection of bone china cups and saucers. Her son Warren made it for her.*

Strawberries - 2008

DIARY ENTRIES—1976

JANUARY 1, 1976—It is New Year's Day—snowy and stormy. We are alone and had one half of a turkey for dinner. Neil listened to the football games. Pa and I saw the floats. They were beautiful.

JANUARY 4, 1976—It is minus thirty this morning. Cold and stormy this afternoon. I finished reading the 'Foxfire' book.
**I had given her the book for a Christmas gift.*

JANUARY 9, 1976—Orrin and Neil went to town and got a vacuum cleaner on approval. I tried it. It is an upright.

JANUARY 11, 1976—Jerry, Ginny and Garth were here. Ginny and I talked about getting the new house drapes and curtains.

JANUARY 15, 1976—Orrin and I went to the new house and cleaned this afternoon. Neil has his bedroom carpet in now. It is pretty.

JANUARY 18, 1976—We couldn't go to Ginny's for Pa's birthday dinner. It was too stormy, but let up towards evening.

JANUARY 23, 1976—There is water in the new house but not hot. Ginny brought up the drapes. Jerry put them up. Jerry and Lou are going to paint the basement floor.

JANUARY 25, 1976—Pa and Neil took the kitchen table over to the new house. We cleaned it first. Pa, Neil, Lou and Jerry painted the basement floor. It looks nice.

JANUARY 28, 1976—Ginny was up and helped with the dishes, putting them in the china cabinet. We started the pantry stuff and Ginny also helped sort things in the upstairs closet.

FEBRUARY 9, 1976—Neil and Jerry took the pump organ down to Jerry's place.
**This is the organ Mother got in a trade with her cousin Winnie Baker. Winnie gave Mother the pump organ and Winnie took Mother's Victrola talking machine (record player). Bakers were moving out West and didn't want the cumbersome organ.*

FEBRUARY 16, 1976—Ginny had her baby girl on the 15th and was about twelve hours in labor. She came feet first. Garth stayed here. They named the baby Muria Joy. She weighed 7 pounds and 4 ounces. She has dark hair.

FEBRUARY 18, 1976—Jerry will meet Yvonne at the Crookston hospital. She will bring her German exchange girl to help Ginny awhile.

FEBRUARY 26, 1976—We moved to the new house. Lou got here in time to help move the refrigerator and stove.

MARCH 8, 1976—Pa and I went to the old house and found some missing items.
**How sad she (the old house) must have felt. Its people abandoned her for a newer model. She's given them the best years of her life—from 1930 to 1976. Mother expresses similar sentiments in her poem about their old home:*

Our Old Home

Our old home was our refuge for forty years.
Leaving it nearly drove me to tears.
The old home cradled two births
They seemed the best on earth.
We observed four anniversaries
One was celebrated in the shade of the trees.
—Ruth Emma Matthews Kruger (1980)

MARCH 20, 1976—The boys moved the china cabinet from the garage to the kitchen. It looks nice.

MARCH 21, 1976—I got the dishes washed and in the china cabinet. It looks nice.

MARCH 22, 1976—We went to Milstein's to Jon and Jane's wedding party. There were a lot of relatives there and they got some lovely gifts. Several pooled their money and bought them a recliner. His mom gave them a pieced quilt.

MARCH 28, 1976—We went to the Farm and Home show banquet at Warren. We saw Jerry get the Outstanding Young Farmer Award. Betty, Mary and Lou were there also.

APRIL 23, 1976—Orrin is planting peas. The boys are planting barley out east.

APRIL 24, 1976—Pa has four potato plants up already.

MAY 16, 1976—It is dry and windy. There are forest fires in northern Minnesota.

MAY 20, 1976—I took the bell tone hearing test. I have 45% hearing loss. I will get an aid for $800. I hope it works.

MAY 21, 1976—I heard from Nancy. She has hypoglycemia or low blood sugar. She needs to follow a diet.
**This was stress-induced hypoglycemia. I had been teaching kindergarten for ten years and working non-stop without a vacation, and it caught up to me. I needed a break, but it never occurred to my doctor or me. My symptoms were depression, weakness, tiredness, and sleeplessness.*

MAY 22, 1976—We may go to Nancy's tomorrow. Then Pa and Neil will go on to Virgil Knaup's at Beaver Dam and then to Uncle Jerry's at Urbana, Illinois in the Winnebago.

MAY 31, 1976—We came home from Nancy's yesterday. We had a good visit. Pa and Neil got back from Virgil's and Uncle Jerry's on Sunday. Virgil is dying of cancer. Uncle Jerry and Eri are about the same.
**This was the last trip for my dad. It was fortunate Neil was endowed with the foresight to realize this.*

JUNE 7, 1976—Jerry got his basement dug for their new house. Ken Knoll will build it.
**This was the year of the drought. There was very little rain.*

JUNE 15, 1976—We heard from Nancy. They will come on Sunday about one or two P.M. They want the Winnebago to take to Lake of the Woods to go fishing on Monday.
**We went to see Betty the next day. We didn't get a first crop of hay and were explaining it to her. "Oh, that's not a problem," she said. Then she pointed to the big Rantanen dairy barn across the road. "They will sell you hay," she said. We considered the trip successful even though we didn't catch any fish.*

JUNE 16, 1976—June had a baby girl born on the 12th.
**This was Jennifer.*

JULY 20, 1976—I got my hearing aid today and I am trying to get used to it. It bothers my ears some.

AUGUST 3, 1976—We saw a Model T Ford on the road today. It looked quaint.

AUGUST 4, 1976—We heard from Nancy. They had several showers of rain so the corn and beans look better.
**I wrote letters weekly until my mother died. She also wrote back and was writing her last letter as she went to the hospital right before she died.*

AUGUST 5, 1976—Jacob swallowed some gasoline at Ted Westlund's place. He's alright now but was in the hospital at Greenbush.

AUGUST 10, 1976—Mary had her baby boy at 11 A.M. She named him Joshua Rantanen Efta. She is at Red Lake Falls hospital. The kids are at Efta's.

AUGUST 11, 1976—We got invited to go to the Richville centennial celebration on August 22. Lydia Ryder Eikert sent the invitation.

AUGUST 14, 1976—We were to see Mary and her new son Joshua Rantanen Efta. He is a nice looking baby—very fair both skin and hair.

AUGUST 22, 1976—Neil, Orrin and I went to the centennial at Richville. Neil took the Winnebago, which has air conditioning. Orrin was asked to speak as an honored guest.

AUGUST 29, 1976—Arne brought Melissa when he came to work. She was here all day until Ginny came about 6 P.M. and took her to their place.

SEPTEMBER 1, 1976—Melissa is very bright and imaginative.

SEPTEMBER 2, 1976—Nancy called in the evening to say "Happy Anniversary."
**It was their fifty-ninth and the last one they would celebrate.

SEPTEMBER 5, 1976—The barn at Jerry's place broke open with the grain stored in it—about 10,000 bushels spilled out onto the ground.

SEPTEMBER 6, 1976—We went to Sabo's wild rice patties near Red Lake Falls on Saturday. When we got back home it had rained .70 of an inch. We were happy to see water again. There was a good rice crop and it was all harvested. The birds got a lot according to Harold Sabo.

SEPTEMBER 20, 1976—Orrin and Neil took in six bags of melons since frost was predicted.

SEPTEMBER 22, 1976—There was a whole page story in the Grand Forks Herald about Ginny and her corn husk dolls and weed decorations. It was a Marilyn Haggerty column.

SEPTEMBER 24, 1976—Lou's Grandma Henke died and her funeral is on Monday.

OCTOBER 4, 1976—Heather got to be Queen of the 3-6 year olds at the Goose Festival in Middle River. She got $25, a board and roses and rode in the parade.
**Heather wasn't too pleased with the board—she wanted the crown!

OCTOBER 16, 1976—Dr. Herber said I should go to Grand Forks to an orthopedic doctor and see about my foot and ankle. Perhaps I should have a brace. It was a terrible dust storm to Thief River Falls. The wind was about fifty miles per hour.

OCTOBER 17, 1976—Orrin cut my hair today. He did a good job. It is too hard to get a date at the Hair Brush.
**I also cut hair for my own family—my kids— until no one wanted my hair cuts any more.

OCTOBER 22, 1976—We froze up seven bags of small carrots today. It was the last of the garden produce.

OCTOBER 26, 1976—Clayton said Betty had fifteen (paying) hunters on Saturday.

NOVEMBER 4, 1976—Neil took Orrin and I to Grand Forks. I went to the orthopedic clinic. He (the specialist) won't do anything for me. He said I should go to the rehab in Grand Forks and get a brace or a special shoe. I might have to stay (there) a week. My cold got a lot worse as it was (both) cold and windy walking up to the clinic.

NOVEMBER 10, 1976—Pa and I wrapped Nancy and Jim's Christmas gift of a Karakul wool blanket. I will send it with Jerry when he goes hunting there tomorrow.

NOVEMBER 16, 1976—Muria is very cute. She rolls all over the floor and tries to creep but goes backwards.

NOVEMBER 17, 1976—We got our Marshall County History book on Friday. It is very interesting. Neil has a write up about us in it. He's also written about Alma Township and the Schey School. Betty wrote about East Valley Township.

NOVEMBER 25, 1976—Pa, Neil and I went to Donna's for Thanksgiving dinner. Heather entertained us by wearing her queen dress from the Middle River Goose Festival and dancing and singing.

DECEMBER 9, 1976—I didn't go to the Homemakers Christmas party at the Lutheran church. Neil went and brought home my present of a felt calendar from Mabel Voytilla.
*Mother doesn't say why she didn't go but obviously didn't feel up to it.

DECEMBER 14, 1976—Neil bought a Christmas tree with long needles. We will set it up soon.
*It must have become too difficult for Betty to cut and bring the traditional fresh-cut tree as in years past.

DECEMBER 21, 1976—It is the shortest day.

DECEMBER 28, 1976—We stopped at Betty's to leave gifts and looked at the work she did on the house. She has a fireplace now and has made the downstairs into two rooms. She has old wood shingles on the wall by the fireplace.

Diary Entries 1977

January 30, 1977—Betty called from near the Old Mill. Her pickup wouldn't go. She wanted Neil to come and get her. Neil couldn't start his car so got Jerry to go with him. When they got where the truck was stalled, it started right away. Betty and Mary wanted to go to the ballet in Grand Forks. Neil wanted to see the Vikings play in the Super-Bowl. He was frustrated.

January 24, 1977—Richard Tangen called and said that Jerry got the State Young Farmer Award at Hawley and will go to Bismarck in March for the national competition.

February 19, 1977—Orrin's amaryllis is blossoming. It has three big white blossoms. It is very beautiful.
**"*An Amaryllis in Winter is Like Money in the Bank*" *was the title of a drawing that I did in pen and ink.*

March 2, 1977—I heard from Nancy. She took a year's leave of absence from teaching at Starbuck.
**I did not go back to teaching in public school again; however, later on I gave art lessons in the home for several years. I was having stress-induced hypoglycemia but didn't realize it at the time. My symptoms were low energy, weakness, and tiredness.*

March 6, 1977—Muria doesn't walk yet but can stand alone one minute.

March 16, 1977—Ruth leaves for Germany on the 22nd and comes back April 5th. She stays with a farm family for five or six days. She goes to Heidelberg, Munich and others. They fly from Bangor, Maine.

March 23, 1977—We saw the article in the Grand Forks Herald about the Jaycees (Young Farmer Award). There were four awards given out. Jerry didn't get one. It was mostly those that were raising cattle, hogs or chickens.

March 24, 1977—Neil and I stopped to look at Jerry and Ginny's house. The bedrooms are large and there are four. They are wall-papered, which is very pretty. There is an open stairway with wrought iron railings. The fireplace is out of the ordinary. It uses stones from the old bridge by the school house in its surround.

April 3, 1977—We got a card from Ruth on her trip with her class in Germany. She was having a good time and was traveling by bus to scenic places.

April 13, 1977—Betty reports that it is very smoky up there (at Middle River). It is from the peat fires that are burning in the refuge.

April 15, 1977—It rained gently all afternoon. It is foggy today. Orrin is planting garden. The grass is getting green.

April 20, 1977—Muria walks now. She is a little unsteady yet, but is cute.

April 24, 1977—It's a lovely day to sit outside. Neil is fixing the lawn mower.

May 1, 1977—We went out east to look around with Neil. Some of the wheat is up. The fields look nice.

May 17, 1977—It was 92 above on May 13th with no rain and very windy. Neil is done planting the sunflowers and is harrowing them now. Jerry and Ginny are moving into their new house.

May 27, 1977—We went to Ethel Grochow's funeral at the Lutheran Church in Warren. A bad storm came up while we were at the service so the committal was at the church.
**Ethel Grochow was one of my mother's long-time friends and a fellow homemaker.*

June 4, 1977—Neil took me to Thief River Falls on May 31st to see Dr. Herber. He thinks it is my gall bladder that is causing my stomach trouble. He gave me new medication. I'm to go back in two weeks.

June 7, 1977—We got back from Mark's reception for his high school graduation. There were between fifty and sixty at the reception. Beaver, Ruth's boyfriend, was there.

June 16, 1977—We saw Arne's girlfriend at Jane's. Diane and Melissa were there too. It was embarrassing for both of them.

June 18, 1977—The Warren Elevator went broke. The boys have $20,000 in it that they lost unless they can collect through their _____? Two hundred farmers lost money and will try to collect something. Nancy and Jim are coming tomorrow and will stay until Monday.
**It was to be my last visit with my dad.*

June 22, 1977—Nancy and Jim were here for Father's Day on June 19th. All of Betty's girls and their kids and spouses were at Ginny's on Sunday.

JULY 3, 1977—Orrin and I went to Ginny's to see about our 60th wedding anniversary. She will call the Methodist Church about it.

JULY 5, 1977—It rained an inch the 2nd of July. We stayed home on the 4th and relaxed at the 4th of July program on the television. It was very good.

JULY 17, 1977—Orrin had a stroke on July 8th. He fell into Neil's arms as he was getting into the car to go to the Warren hospital. He got sick Thursday evening and was sick most of the night with a pain in his arm. They took Orrin by ambulance to the Grand Forks hospital. He is in a coma. We went to see him yesterday. He has a normal temperature.
**Orrin would not allow Neil to take him to the hospital the previous evening—thinking it would pass, that it was a false alarm, or perhaps he thought this is IT and an easy way out.*

JULY 19, 1977—Betty, Neil and I went to the hospital. Nancy came last Saturday. She stayed until Wednesday the 13th. Neil took her home.
**The reason Neil took me home was that Jim arranged to have me flown to Warren in a small, private plane. My car wasn't safe to drive the 210 miles (to Warren). The plane landed at the Marshall County fair grounds, and Neil and Jerry met me there.*

JULY 21, 1977—We are going to the Homemakers picnic at Anna Thorson's. We will tour the old log cabin.
**This was the log cabin built by Henrick and Ingeborg Schey in 1880 on the banks of the Middle River in Alma Township. It still stands there as I write this notation.*

JULY 22, 1977—Mary took me to Grand Forks to the hospital to see Orrin. He was the same. No temperature. The Dr. said they should remove the I.V. If they remove it from him he won't last long. He has no movement and his eyes are always closed. The boys (Neil and Jerry) will ask the girls (Betty and Nancy) what to do. Betty is coming tonight. I didn't want to say anything (either way).

JULY 29, 1977—Orrin's funeral was last Sunday, July 24th. He died on July 22nd. He never regained consciousness after the stroke.

AUGUST 1, 1977—Orrin had a big funeral with military ceremonies both at the church and cemetery. I am very sad and lonesome.
**My father loved his plants and flowers. This poem is dedicated to him:*

Flowers

I went out cutting flowers.
To a meadow on the hill.
I spied a riot of colors
Every desire to fulfill.

Some were tame,
Cultivated, mild.

Others different,
Rare, unusual, wild!

If I were a flower,
Which one would I be?
The Unexpected wild flower,
Or the tame variety?

—Nancy A. Olson, July 22, 1977

AUGUST 1, 1977—The children and friends have been most kind. Nancy brought her own flowers.

**I made an arrangement of zinnias and marigolds with some wild flowers. My father so loved his gardens. I thought homegrown flowers were most appropriate.*

AUGUST 4, 1977—It rains a little almost every night. It is lonesome without Orrin.

AUGUST 9, 1977--A lovely day. We were to Mary's yesterday to Joshua's first birthday.

AUGUST 13, 1977—Lydia Eckert called and wanted us to come to an old timer's picnic at Richville on Sunday. She was surprised when I told her Orrin was dead.

AUGUST 27, 1977—The boys finished combining on the 24th. It is a record. Mary came over and vacuumed the carpets and cleaned the bathroom.

SEPTEMBER 7, 1977—It is very lonesome without Orrin.

SEPTEMBER 15, 1977—Neil and I got back from Nancy and Jim's on the 11th. We had a lovely visit at Nancy's. Jim took us to the A and W Drive in for supper on Saturday. We saw lovely scenery on the trip to Nancy's.

OCTOBER 13, 1977—Betty called to tell me about Orrin's obituary being in the Farmer magazine this week.

NOVEMBER 1, 1977—We had Garth, Muria, Joe, Jacob, and Nancy Nichols for tricks and treats last night. Muria and Garth looked so cute in their pillow slip costumes…as were Joe and Jacob.

NOVEMBER 3, 1977—Betty called to say that Arne and Diane got married again on October 8th.

NOVEMBER 9, 1977—We have about four inches of new snow.

NOVEMBER 24, 1977—Neil and I went to Donna's for Thanksgiving dinner. There is a lot of snow up that way. The spruce and evergreen (trees) were a sight to behold. It was a nice day.

DECEMBER 6, 1977—I have been writing Christmas cards every day and wrapped gifts and baked cookies today.

**Mother is eighty years old. Death had claimed her husband and yet she continued. She realized these activities gave her a purpose, centered her in the moment, and provided goals for that day.

DECEMBER 20, 1977—Neil bought me a poinsettia. It is very pretty.

Hen and Chicks - 2001

Diary Entries 1978

(The Diaries are limited to a few entries in 1978…The first one is January 31, 1978).

January 31, 1978—Betty was here in the afternoon and she stayed for supper. We had a good visit.

February 2, 1978—Neil took me to Anna Thorson's for Homemaker's on February 1st. It was a nice day. Ten members were there. The lesson was on salads. The boys are hauling barley to Red Lake Falls.

February 5, 1978—Neil and Jerry ordered Orrin a tombstone yesterday from Delwin Potucek. The stone is maroon and black in color. It was an engraving of flowers on the side and our names in the middle.

March 3, 1978—Neil took me to Ella Bjorgaard's for Homemaker's. Ernest Bjorgaard and his wife were there. They were very entertaining. He has a southern drawl.
**I met Ernest when Jim and I visited our daughter Ruth in Lenexa, Kansas.*

March 5, 1978—I gave Ginny one of the pictures of the General Store at Richville. She was pleased to get it.

March 15, 1978—Nancy writes that Joyce Elvehjem had a big black haired baby boy. She will give it up for adoption through the Lutheran Social Services.
**My daughter Ruth went to the hospital in Glenwood and stayed with Joyce through her labor and delivery. When she was discharged from the hospital, I picked her up and was with her when she handed over the baby to the Lutheran Social Service worker. She came home with me and we sat on the sofa and visited awhile. I was feeling at a loss in this new difficult situation, but perhaps in some small measure helped her through this painful transition in her young life. This poem was written for Joyce as she gave up her baby boy:*

She

She had a tiny baby boy.
She held him...
She looked at him...
She loved him...
She let him go.

She had a tiny baby child.
I held her baby for her.
To tenderly give away.
I watched the tears...
I tried to share...
To care...
To reason—Why, Why?

She had a tiny baby.
It has been many years now.
She still waits to hold...
She still thinks about...
She still wants to shout,
'THAT IS MY BABY!'

Some day, I pray, that baby
May know that 'she,' had a baby 'him,'
That 'she' loved him tenderly,
And with so much longing, let him go...
So that he might grow strong with
ANOTHER.

She had a tiny baby boy,
She held him and then—
Let him go."

—By Nancy A. Olson

MARCH 27, 1978—Jon and Jane are moving to Hallock. He will work for a big farm for $750 a month.

MARCH 28, 1978—Mary had a big seven-pound boy at the Thief River Falls hospital. She hasn't named him yet.

MEMORIAL Day, 1978—We went to the cemetery last night. The monument (for Orrin and me) looks good.

June 7, 1978—Betty was here. She has had all her teeth out but five. She looks very peaked and can scarcely talk. She is putting in a bathroom soon. Eddie Lien may do (it) for $5,000.

June 20, 1978—Betty still has four teeth to pull.

July 11, 1978—Nancy and Jim came on the 6th and left in the afternoon of the 7th. Neil and Lou took Jim to Lake of the Woods fishing on Saturday. They got a nice mess of fish.

July 22, 1978—Orrin died one year ago today. It has been a lonesome year for me…even though there is family (nearby). This is fair time. Neil went to work in the _____? booth.

July 26, 1978—Orrin's funeral was one year ago.

August 10, 1978—Donna, June and the kids were here yesterday. Donna has hypoglycemia (low blood sugar).
**This is the condition diagnosed by my doctor (approximately this same time) who said, "You can't possibly have such a low reading without a cause. You must have a tumor on your pancreas." (In other words—"you'll be pushing up daisies before long.")*

August 20, 1978—Mary took me to Betty's on Friday afternoon. Eddie Lien was installing her tub. It is blue. Betty gave us pie for lunch. Betty looks quite well.

August 24, 1978—Jane, Tasha and Ivan were here on the 22nd. They live at Hallock. She is expecting her baby in December.

October 20, 1978—Betty was here on the 16th and got $20 worth of wild rice. Jim, Dale and Lowell (Olson) are coming to hunt on the 18th.

October 30, 1978—Neil had a letter from Eri saying Uncle Jerry had a massive stroke two weeks ago. He is in a coma.

November 1, 1978—Arne and Jane have a baby boy born on Betty's birthday, October 28th. Neil called Betty to tell her about Uncle Jerry.
**This was Arne III.*

November 5, 1978—Uncle Jerry died yesterday at 5 a.m. There is no funeral or memorial services. He will be cremated and buried in the cemetery at Wadena near his parents' (grandparents' and great-great-grandparents') graves.

November 10, 1978—Jerry and Ginny stopped at the Wadena cemetery on their way to Nancy's. They hadn't buried his remains. It was snowing and a bad day.

December 9, 1978—Neil took me to the Homemaker's Christmas party at the Alma Lutheran Church on the 7th. There was a feast of food and we played Bingo. I have been writing Christmas cards and received quite a few.

DECEMBER 26, 1978—Neil and I were to Ginny's and Jerry's for Christmas Eve supper. Muria got five dolls. Neil gave Garth an electric train. We had a big supper: lutefisk, lefsa, rice pudding, baked potatoes, buns, plum pudding, and coffee.

DECEMBER 31, 1978—The Carolers were here on Friday and left a big box of goodies. Nancy writes that Mark had a knee injury (from playing soccer). He came home from Florida and will go to St. Cloud for surgery. He came home by bus, which took 51 hours. He was cold and sick.

Diary Entries 1979

January 1, 1979—The big news is that Jane had her baby girl at 2 A.M. on New Year's morning at Karlstad and named her Lacey.

January 7, 1979—We heard from Eri yesterday. She is going to Florida on January 28th and will stay for two months.

January 11, 1979—Nancy writes that Jim had a rabid steer that he had to shoot. The vet thought a skunk bit it.

**This by no means was the end of the rabid animals at our farm. Later there was another steer that acted strange at night and by morning had to be shot. And then there was the rabid cat that bit me. We didn't realize the cat was rabid until seven days after the bite, which caused quite a bit of anxiety until I got the gamma globulin and the vaccine into me.

January 16, 1979—It is Orrin's birthday and a bad stormy one. He would have been 84 if he had lived.

**My dad's favorite story about his birth was that his parents were living in a poorly insulated chicken house. It was so cold the night he was born that his father had to stand holding him near the stove so he wouldn't freeze to death.

January 17, 1979—Neil and I had to baby-sit Garth and Muria on Sunday afternoon. The kids were quite good. I told them stories and they turned somersaults for us.

January 19, 1979—Ruth writes that she has a job three days a week. Nancy writes that Mark's knee is better and he will go to St. Cloud to see the doctor.

February 20, 1979—There was a total eclipse of the sun yesterday. It was not total here. Jerry, Ginny, Lou, Mary and the kids went to _____? Canada, where it was total.

MARCH 7, 1979—I was to the doctor on the 5th for my stomach. I got very sick from riding in the car. The nurses wanted to put me in the hospital. Dr. Pumela gave me Tagament...I think he thought I had ulcers.

MARCH 13, 1979—President Carter got back from Israel and Egypt, but there was no peace accord.

APRIL 3, 1979—We went to Nancy's on March 31 and came back on April 2. Alan was home from the hospital in St. Cloud. He will come home and stay on April 4 and then go back to school.

APRIL 9, 1979—Jon Hirst stopped awhile on Wednesday. He had been to Argyle to get seed cleaned. He said Jane works at the Pembina bus factory from 4:30 P.M. to 12:30 A.M. He baby sits or they get a girl.

APRIL 17, 1979—We were at Jerry and Ginny's for Easter. Jerry came and got us in his four-wheel drive pickup. The roads were impassible otherwise.

APRIL 18, 1979—Jerry went to town yesterday (with the four-wheel drive pickup) and got the mail. The mail hadn't been gone for three days.

APRIL 19, 1979—Warren has a flood. There is 5 feet of water in some places and no travel in or out of town and no mail. There was a crew of men working at Gladys Bagaas's place this morning sandbagging to keep the water out.

APRIL 24, 1979—It rained all day. Everything is wet again. There is water in the basement of the house. Grand Forks and East Grand Forks have the worst flood of the century. The sandbag dikes aren't able to hold (back the water). Oslo is also flooded. A thousand or more people had to leave their homes in Grand Forks...including the residents of St. Agnes guest home.

APRIL 30, 1979—It is cold and cloudy today but no rain. The flood has gone to the north. It is all flooded from the border to Winnipeg, Canada. Several thousand farm families had to leave their homes. Pembina is flooded. Jane and Jon postponed Lacey's baptism until a later date. We had a letter from Eri today. She wants Neil to pick out a marker or headstone for Uncle Jerry. She will pay for it.
**The flood of 1997 was exceptionally destructive with Grand Forks looking like a war zone under siege with both fire and water or as someone termed in the title of a book about it, Come Hell and High Water. This led to the federally funded flood diversion projects for Warren, Grand Forks and East Grand Forks.*

MAY 4, 1979—It is still cloudy and cold. It was 27 degrees above this morning. The boys got their air seeder from Langdon. It cost $25,000. I hope they can use it. There is water in the basement yet. Neil tries to pump it out. Jane and Jon had to move out of their home near Pembina because of the flood. They went to his mother's house at Williams.

MAY 5, 1979—Jean Brosdahl Knutson had to come out of her place by boat to go to her uncle's funeral at Viking. Jens Hunstad died. He was eighty-nine years old.

MAY 19, 1979—The boys are working like mad to get the field work done. They are out east now.

MAY 28, 1979—This is a warm windy day. Yesterday Ginny, Garth, Muria and I went to the cemetery to Orrin's grave. Ginny planted some petunias on it. The cemetery looked beautiful…so clean and green and well kept. Ginny told us the good news that she is pregnant…and said it was unplanned.

MAY29, 1979—The grass is getting long and should be mowed. The "Big Tree" looks beautiful—so fresh and green.
**This is a revision of a poem my mother wrote about the "Box Elder Tree." It was always called the "Big Tree," so that is what I will call it.*

The Big Tree

The Big Tree grew in our yard.
It was an object of pride…
And pleasure. A cool place
Especially in the hottest weather.
Orrin said, 'fairies live there.'
With branches sturdy and leaves so fair.

—Revised by Nancy A. Olson

JUNE 8, 1979—Mary took me to Betty's one afternoon. It is so wet there on her land because the (officials) at the (Mud Lake) refuge opened the flood gates so the water (spilled) out onto her land. We saw Betty's four goats, one cow, one horse, and some sheep and a peacock. I heard from Nancy. She was chosen to be on jury duty in a power line case at Glenwood, (a criminal suit) against a man named William T. Hansen from Wadena.
**This lawsuit was a result of an ongoing protest against a power line being built north of Glenwood, starting in North Dakota and ending in the Twin Cities. It was an unforgettable experience.*

JUNE 17, 1979—Father's Day. Neil took me to the doctor in Thief River Falls. He said I should have a bone operation on my foot. We have to set a date for it. The operation will cost $1,000 dollars.

JUNE 21, 1979—The first day of summer—cool and damp. The orthopedic surgeon said he wouldn't operate on my foot. My bones are too brittle. He advised me to have a special shoe made…costing about $200. We saw June and family at the clinic. Tony had to get twenty-two stitches out. He had fallen in the basement.
**Tony inherited the easily torn skin that is possessed by both my mother Ruth and sister Betty. There is a technical name for it and it is definitely inherited.*

July 15, 1979—Jerry saw about the marker or monument for Uncle Jerry. It will cost $750 installed. Eri has lung cancer and will have surgery for it soon. She doesn't want to have chemotherapy if they can't get it all. She doesn't care if she lives or dies.

July 29, 1979—Don Loeslie, Jerry's neighbor, had a big barbecue at their place on Friday evening. Governor Al Quie was honored guest. He shook Neil's hand. There were about 100 people there. They were served roast pig, salad and corn on the cob.

Augsut 2, 1979—Nancy sold one of her paintings at the Glenwood Waterama.
**This was the beginning of my life as an artist.*

August 7, 1979—Eri called on Saturday evening. She is out of the hospital but has pain and can't talk much.

August 20, 1979—Nancy writes they are leaving for Indiana and Illinois on August 30.
**It was a memorable trip. We visited Ray and Nina Musselman at their farm in Indiana. They are Jan's parents. Jan was married to Jim's brother, Dale Olson. They were pleasant and sociable people and showed us farming in Indiana. Ray was a representative to the Indiana legislature. Eri was recovering from her lung cancer surgery and pleased to have company.*

September 23, 1979—It is a lovely day. We got my (custom made) shoes on Friday from Grand Forks. I was disappointed in them. I can't put them on alone...and there is no foam rubber inside like there should be.

September 27, 1979—I fell by the refrigerator about 4 p.m. and had to sit on the floor until 9 p.m. when Neil came home. I hunched myself along into the living room (to get on the carpet). It was grueling.

September 28, 1979—Jane and the kids were here yesterday for dinner. The baby is cute (Lacey) with her red hair. She slides around on her stomach.

October 13, 1979—Neil phoned the foot Dr. yesterday. He said I had the worst arthritic feet he'd ever seen on the x-ray. He won't operate on the one that has a spur on the bone. He said it could come back again in six months.

October 21, 1979—We had Gladys Bagaas (over) to do the cleaning on Wednesday and Saturday. She cleaned the refrigerator and stove and vacuumed the living room carpet. When I got up this morning, the grain dryer was on fire. I called Neil and he got the fire department from Argyle. They put the fire out quickly but there was a lot of damage.

November 5, 1979—The snow is mostly gone, but it is gloomy...depressing weather. I fell yesterday afternoon and hit my head and hurt my knee and neck. It is somewhat better this morning. No one came for tricks or treats but Muria and Garth. Muria was a witch and Garth was a lion.

November 17, 1979—Ginny had her baby on Saturday, November 17th by Caesarean section. It is a girl weighing 8 pounds. Ginny named the baby Meredith Leigh.

November 26, 1979—Jerry was going after Ginny and Meredith on Saturday when Andy Morkassel ran into the front of Jerry's car. It was totaled out. Muria and Garth were along. No one was hurt which is something to be thankful for.

December 1, 1979—I fell last Tuesday in the bedroom and have a black eye. Muria and Garth were here on Saturday morning. Ginny went to work at the hospital.

December 5, 1979—Neil took me to the doctor on Monday. He said I was anemic and I have to take iron pills…and will have to take blood pressure pills for two weeks. I got the walker. It goes good.

December 23, 1979—Neil went to Jane's and Jon's near Newfolden. I was too sick on my stomach and bowels so I couldn't go. Jerry stayed with me for about two hours.
**I don't suppose taking an iron pill helped my mother's stomach problem.

December 27, 1979—Betty was here for dinner on Christmas. Jerry, Ginny and family came and brought the dinner. Betty brought a hot dish. Meredith looked cute in a Santa Claus suit. Neil helped Garth build a crane (with an erector set).

Diary Entries 1980

JANUARY 9, 1980—I went to the hospital for diarrhea a week ago Saturday and was there for nine days. I came home on Monday, the 7th. I had Mrs. McFarland for a roommate. She was a case and a half to live with. The clan visited almost every day.

FEBRUARY 29, 1980—It was minus 35 below this morning. I got home from the hospital on Monday. Mrs. Julia Shimpa of Greenbush is staying here. She is quite competent. Jane and Jon were here yesterday. He bought the farm at Newfolden. Julia had baked rolls so all had plenty to eat.
**Julia was hired to take care of my mother.*

MARCH 12, 1980—Julia got back but wants to leave before the 19th to babysit her granddaughter's kids while she has an operation. Jane phoned Neil that she would keep me instead of going to St. Vincent's rest home on Monday (it was at Crookston). I am afraid of their smoke (Jane and Jon smoked cigarettes) and the kids. Betty was here yesterday while Julia went home. Nancy may come this weekend. Nancy is coming today with the trucker (Buster Faulkner) who is getting a load of seed wheat.
**It is the only time I've taken a trip in the sleeper in the back of the truck cab.*

MARCH 17, 1980—St. Patrick's Day. Neil and Nancy brought me to the St. Vincent's today. Neil went on to Nancy's and took her home. I just had dinner and it was the worst looking group of people I have ever seen, but I ate anyway. The room is pleasant and sunny. We brought lots of things from home like pictures and pillows and books. Neil brought me a television set which is very nice.
**This was the situation: Most all of the residents of St. Vincent's had Alzheimer's or similar aging illnesses. My mother was alert and completely lucid to the very end of her life. After realizing that there would not be anyone with whom to have an intelligent conversation, she demanded to be taken out of that place. It looks by the diary entries that she was there a month.*

MARCH 22, 1980—Mary and baby daughter, Amber, and Lou were here yesterday. The baby is so cute...like a little flower. She will be baptized perhaps on Easter Sunday.

127

MARCH 23, 1980—It was Sunday and a lonesome day. Two nuns came to see me. They are friendly people. I wrote to Corrine (Hickey) today. I got my first letters here...one from Nancy and one from Min Gunnerson. There are robins at Glenwood...none here.

MARCH 26, 1980—St. Vincent's, Crookston. It snowed two or three inches but it is melting (now). I went to a sing along yesterday. It was real good. They sang World War One songs and others.

MARCH 28, 1980—St. Vincent's—Crookston. The Rev. Clausen of the Warren Methodist church came to see me yesterday afternoon. We had a good visit. I did most of the talking. It is a lovely day and has thawed a lot.

APRIL 11, 1980—St. Vincent's—Crookston. I went to the protestant church services at St. Francis chapel here. It is snowing like rain.

APRIL 17, 1980—Neil moved me here to Jane's at Newfolden on the 15th. It is nice, pleasant and sunny here. The house has eight rooms. Jane has (house) plants. Jane does well to take care of me, foot and all.

APRIL 18, 1980—Jane's—Newfolden. It is a nice day. There are some big trees here. One must be about one hundred years old. Jon traps gophers and gets as many as nine some days. The home health nurse was here and looked at my foot.

APRIL 19, 1980—Neil phoned and said I could be admitted to the Good Samaritan (nursing home) next Tuesday.

APRIL 22, 1980—Jane's at Newfolden. Jane had Neil, Betty, June, Clayton and three kids, Donna, Armand and two kids for dinner and lunch. We sat in her lovely yard all afternoon. There are many big trees.

APRIL 26, 1980—Neil brought me to the Good Samaritan home on Tuesday in a black (dirt) blizzard. Mrs. Mabel Wood is my roommate. She is blind. The room is nice and comfortable.

MAY 1, 1980—This is May Day. The handyman mowed the grass this morning. It had been watered. It is very warm.

MAY 5, 1980—It was 95 above yesterday. Neil came after dinner and brought me two summer dresses and the newspaper and magazines.

MAY 12, 1980—It was Mother's Day yesterday. Nancy came on Saturday and brought me our wedding certificate framed with our family picture in it. Neil came and got me early on Sunday morning and took me home. Ginny brought the dinner: chicken, dressing, buns, fruit salad, potatoes and vegetables. We had rhubarb pie and ice cream for dessert. Betty came and brought cowslips. Muria brought me lilacs. Neil brought me back at 7:30 P.M. I had a good time and visit.

MAY 13, 1980—Armand Westlund came to the dining room and told me about the baby girl Donna had on Sunday evening of Mother's Day. It was a big one…eight pounds or more.
**This was Nicolette.*

MAY 17, 1980—No rain.

MAY 19, 1980—No rain. It was 80 above and sultry. Neil came and took me to the cemetery. The grass is drying up. There is a little peony on Pa's grave. It was nice to get outside.

MAY 22, 1980—It is very hot. It was 96 degrees above yesterday and 100 is predicted for Grand Forks today. Neilo Rantanen died.

MAY 27, 1980—Memorial Day was the 26th…no company. It rained a small shower in the morning. Betty, Jerry and Neil were here on Sunday the 25th.

JUNE 2, 1980—It rained a shower of ¼ inch at home.

JUNE 3, 1980—The old house is being torn down. Lou wants the furnace. Jerry took the twenty-gallon stone crock. The bathtub stands out of doors. The inside of the house is gone.

JUNE 11, 1980—Ginny made and gave me a pocket for my combs, books and magazines. The pockets hang on (the sides of) my chair so that I can easily reach my things.

JUNE 16, 1980—Neil, Betty and I went to Wadena on Saturday to see the six Kruger graves—Michael Kruger, Wilhelmine Riemann Kruger, August Kruger, Wilhelm Frederick Kruger, Minnie Knaup Kruger and Peter Gerald Kruger. On Sunday we went to the Deer Creek cemeteries…we saw my grandparents' graves—Nancy Powers Matthews and Jacob Matthews at the old cemetery (North of the village), Adelia Matthews Tuffs and James Tuffs and Lou Matthews Gard and James Gard at the other cemetery. They are my aunts and uncles.
**We can't find a headstone for Jacob Matthews at the old cemetery north of Deer Creek.*

JUNE 17, 1980—There was a terrific hail storm on Friday night. It broke my window plus thirty-five other windows. The hail was golf ball in size. We had to move out into the hall so the glass could be cleaned up. The glass blew all over and covered my head.

JUNE 28, 1980—It rained last night—2.1 inches of rain. It was a welcome rain. I sit at a different table now…near a side window.

JULY 3, 1980—We had a picnic in the park last night. We went in the bus to the fairgrounds. We had a sack lunch. The bus that took us has a wheel chair lift. It was fun to go. The bus was full.

JULY 7, 1980—Neil took me to the big one and a half hour parade on Saturday. It had very beautiful floats…many horses and 1400 or so people participating. We watched from the car (which Neil parked) by the fairgrounds.

July 17, 1980—I was nominated to be one of the queen candidates of the Good Samaritan Home yesterday…not that it means anything. The fair begins.

July 31, 1980—I had a letter from Nancy. They are combining now.

August 4, 1980—We practiced for the ice-cream social program. It went well.

August 8, 1980—I didn't get to be Queen of the Good Samaritan home. Mrs. Mary Meruska got the honor. She is ninety years old. She sang "America the Beautiful." I recited "The Village Blacksmith," and got lots of compliments for it.
**Mother had a phenomenal memory. I remember her reciting poetry. "The Village Blacksmith" was one of her favorite pieces.*

August 14, 1980—The Republican Convention elected Ronald Reagan to run for president. The Democrats elected Jimmy Carter. Ted Kennedy wouldn't run.

August 15, 1980—I heard from Nancy. She and Jim will be up here the weekend of August 23 and 24. They are going on a trip to Glacier Park. They will start by driving across Canada and then come down into the United States through Glacier Park and then on to Montana and back home.

August 18, 1980—Jerry, Neil and Garth were here yesterday. They had 1500 acres to combine yet. Neil dried the grain and was very tired.

August 25, 1980—Neil came and took me home on Sunday. Nancy and Jim stopped to see me on Saturday and brought me flowers. Everyone came on Sunday including Jerry, Ginny and their children, Mary, Lou and children, and Betty.

August 26, 1980—I came back to the Good Samaritan Home this morning at 8:30. Nancy helped me sort out some winter clothes. Jim and Nancy left for Regina, Saskatchewan.

August 28, 1980—Garth started school today and is in the first grade. He had his bag along. Ginny made it. He showed us what he did in school. The women in the dining room all seemed happy to see the children—especially Meredith who was creeping.

September 1, 1980—Today was our wedding anniversary. We would have been married sixty-three years if Orrin hadn't died three years ago on the 22nd of July. Jerry and Ginny and family stopped here yesterday on their way to Tangen's at Hawley. Ginny left me a piece of apple pie.

September 2, 1980—I heard from Nancy. They were in Glacier Park on Wednesday and slept in a tent…on Tuesday evening. It was chilly (and had snowed in the mountains that night). They saw a bear cross the road. They also stopped at Jim's Uncle Paul and Aunt Pearl Morton's in Montana.

SEPTEMBER 8, 1980—Neil was here yesterday afternoon and read Nancy's letter describing their trip to Canada and Glacier Park. It must have been wonderful and exciting.

**It was an exceptionally memorable trip. For one thing, it is the only time I slept in a tent, and I also remember how the mountains looked. The song, "America the Beautiful" has a line that poetically describes them—"purple mountain's majesty above the fruited plains." I remember writing about this part of the trip in particular since it was the first, last, and only time that we drove out West and saw the mountains appear in the distance. It is lovely to know all these years hence how much my mother enjoyed our trip vicariously.

SEPTEMBER 27, 1980—I went to the Old Mill on the Home bus. It was a lovely day and the trees were beautiful in autumn colors…some red and others yellow.

SEPTEMBER 30, 1980—Ruth Johnson, Anna Thorson and her aunt were here to see Mabel Wood, my roommate, on Sunday. Mabel is the only girl left from a family of ten girls in a family of twelve. She was a teacher.

OCTOBER 11, 1980—Mabel Wood got a flu shot and won't eat today. She just sleeps all the time.
**Mother watched over Mabel, rang the bell for her, and was her friend.

OCTOBER 15, 1980—The handbell ringers—women from Grand Forks and Alvarado—gave us a concert in the solarium while we ate dinner. It was quite good.

OCTOBER 19, 1980—I heard from granddaughter, Ruth Olson. She works in a radio station in Duluth, playing records and gives the news and weather. Neil was here on Friday and said that Mary and Lou are building a house. It will be done by March first.

OCTOBER 24, 1980—I had two turkeys looking in my window yesterday. There were five of them. They are wild turkeys of Harry Howard's.
**The turkey was one of the birds my father raised to make money in addition to the dairy cows. We always had a freshly butchered turkey for Thanksgiving and a freshly butchered goose for Christmas.

NOVEMBER 5, 1980—Ronald Reagan is our new president. He was elected by a big majority. I am reading "The Hiding Place."

NOVEMBER 12, 1980—Debbie Stinar wants me to have a private room that Mrs. Haugaard was in. I will ask Neil about it. I didn't think I would like it. It would be too lonely.

NOVEMBER 18, 1980—Lovely day. Neil, Betty and Nancy leave for Urbana today. They will stop at Fox Lake, Wisconsin, to see Forest Knaup (Dad's cousin).
**Forest was a charming, elderly gentleman who had red hair at one time. As a child he went by the nickname of Topsy. Being a visually oriented person, I remember the landscape and the glorious weathered classic barns along the back roads that took us to Fox Lake. Nearing sunset the sky bounced the pinks, oranges, reds and mauves into the shadows on those buildings. It is something I'll always remember… and always remember that I had no camera.

DECEMBER 17, 1980—It is Garth's birthday. He is seven. Ginny will have seven boys from the bus for a party. She brought a big bunch of holly for Mabel and me.

DECEMBER 26, 1980—Neil took me out (to the farm) on Christmas day for dinner. Ginny brought roast goose, cranberries, lefsa, cinnamon bread, whole wheat bread, peas, asparagus, fruit soup, Swedish rice, mashed potatoes, tea, coffee and plum pudding.

Diary Entries 1981

January 5, 1981—Eri died on January 2nd. Neil, Jerry and Nancy left for Illinois on the 4th of January to sort the household effects, begin to settle up the estate, and hear the will read. They will be back on the 10th. Eri had a heart attack at the clinic.

**The trip to Urbana, Illinois, was somewhat grueling. Neil caught a nasty cold and was miserable. Jerry hated the cigarette smoke that had permeated Eri's house and furniture, and I couldn't sleep in that spooky setting. I needed an Ambien, but it was before the time of that sleeping aid. Consequently, we were running on empty; but in spite of our shortcomings, we thoroughly and carefully sorted the contents of Uncle Jerry and Eri's home. We saved all the memorabilia, gave articles that we could not use to the Salvation Army, and packed the U-Haul with what we kept. As I write this, I am using a tool of Eri's on a daily basis. It is a gradated hand wrench to open bottle screw caps.*

January 13, 1981—Nancy, Jerry and Neil got back safely from Illinois with the U-Haul. There were sets of dishes, furniture, jewelry, and clothing. It will be divided on January 25 when Nancy and Jim come. Neil took the refrigerator table and couch. The couch smells of cigarette smoke. Neil found in Uncle Jerry's papers a letter about mountain climbing in Europe. There are a lot of papers to go through.

**I spent years sorting, copying, and editing the letters for my book, We Flew With Our Own Wings. The letters were eventually donated to various libraries around the country. The two most noteworthy libraries are the Karl Kroch at Cornell University in Ithaca, New York, and the Bancroft at the University of California, Berkeley.*

January 26, 1981—Nancy and Jim will come today to help distribute Eri's things. I was there yesterday to see them. There is a bedroom full and a big table in the basement is full of dishes. Jerry got Lloyd George Melgaard to appraise the dishes. There were two lovely vases. There were many articles of clothing and jewelry.

**I had the jewelry appraised and we took turns rotating—who had the first choice in which round. We settled without any major disputes. Jim and Lou went fishing.*

February 12, 1981—Roy Wood and his daughter and baby were here to see Mabel. She took many pictures of Mabel and the baby.

February 27, 1981—It was Mabel's birthday yesterday. She was 94 years old. Harriet gave her a party and had the relatives.

March 5, 1981—Mary invited Neil and I to Joe's first communion on March 15.

March 6, 1981—Jerry received the sad news that Richard Tangen of Hawley was killed in a power take off accident yesterday. The funeral is Tuesday. He is the father of four children ages 3-11, and one is on the way (Richelle).

March 16, 1981—It is a lovely day. Neil took me to Mary's on Sunday for Joe's First Communion. The priest was there and led the program of readings. Sandra Nowaski led the singing.

March 20, 1981—Nancy writes that Mark and Jim rented a farm from a widow (Donna Knutson). Mark gets one-third, Jim one-third, and Donna one-third. It is the first day of spring. We have sunshine and snow...only a few snow banks.

April (?) 1981—We woke up to a light snowfall. It soon melted.

April 13, 1981—Yesterday was Palm Sunday. Neil took me to Betty's yesterday. Betty has lambs, two geese and some cows.

May 13, 1981—Nancy was home for Mother's day. She came on Friday and went back on Monday morning. She brought me a lovely bouquet of crab-apple blossoms. Nancy brought along pictures of Eri. Neil had the letters Uncle Jerry had written to her for us to read. It was all so very interesting. We had a good time discussing them.
**Uncle Jerry used "Puppichen" or "Puppi" as the salutation at the beginning of his letters.*

May 18, 1981—It is a lovely day. I would like to be outside. The dandelions are thick here in the yard. Neil was here yesterday.

May 22, 1981—It has been very hot here. I hope Neil comes today and puts up the fan.

May 25, 1981—It is Memorial Day. It is cloudy and rainy. It rained four inches in a cloud burst on Saturday out east on the Peterson, Klopp and Underbakke places. Neil took me to the cemetery to see Orrin's grave. Mary put a bunch of yellow flowers on it.

May 30, 1981—Mary and five kids were here about an hour. Amber is getting cute and gets into mischief.

June 3, 1981—Deb Stinar and Leona Negaard were here yesterday and wanted Mabel to move down near the dining room and other nurses station...but she won't do it. They want me to move down that way but I don't want to go...So I will have to put up with Mabel.

June 23, 1981—Sunday. Neil took me out home. It was raining but stopped long enough so I didn't get wet. I looked at the peony buds, the yard, the big tree, scrapbooks, photo- albums. I enjoyed myself! Neil has three telephones in the house.
*When I was living at home we did not have a telephone.

July 10, 1981—Mary and the kids were here last evening. We went outside and sat awhile. It was lovely. Amber climbed around on the picnic table.

August 5, 1981—It is smoky today. There are fires in Canada. It is so dry there. Joyce Elvehjem had a nice wedding in the (Morning Glory Gardens) and it didn't rain.

August 17, 1981—Neil came on Friday. He said they have 140 acres yet to combine. It went slow because the grain is so heavy. They can only do 15 acres in a day. It gets to be 40 above at night so it is cool. The daytime temps are in the 70s.
*There were two exceptionally cool years in the early 1980s, which were good for small grains like wheat but not compatible with the crops that required heat units like corn and beans. Later on we learned that, at least in part, this dramatic weather shift was attributed to the volcanic ash particles in the air from an eruption of Mt. St. Helens. Our crops were poor from the lack of heat.

August 18, 1981—The Grand Forks Herald reports the farmers who had grain stored in the Warren elevator will get their money back that was lost when the elevator went broke and 6 percent interest. The judge ruled that Cargill has to pay for their loss.

September 5, 1981—Neil took me home for a walleye dinner on Thursday. It was very good fish. We also had baked potatoes and jell-o.
*My husband Jim caught the fish. He continues to be recognized for his ability to catch the finny creatures. He only fished for walleyes and gave most of them away.

September 14, 1981—Yesterday was grandparents day. I had my picture taken at the Good Samaritan with most of my grandchildren.

September 26, 1981—Corrine Hickey sent me a clipping from the newspaper about her granddaughter, Lori. She is teaching four pupils in a new school in the Badlands…thirty-four miles from Medora. She lives in the schoolhouse.

October 5, 1981—It is a rainy day with some snow forecast for tonight. Betty had forty hunters for the opening of goose season.

October 19, 1981—The Allspice singing group was at the center yesterday and sang. Ginny was the master of ceremonies. Muria was along and sat by me while the program went on.

October 23, 1981—I got an unusual card saying that Ron Olson's friend, Herbert Greggs had died. He was fifty years old, a dancer, actor and artist.
*Herbert's death was attributed to Hepatitis B. Herbert was originally from Haiti. Ron met him in New York while working for Century Lighting Company.

November 1, 1981—Yesterday the center had a big Halloween party with costumes and all. They were very gay and astonishing. My nurse's aid was Little Red Riding Hood.

December 3, 1981—Nancy writes that she had a big Thanksgiving. She had Warren, Pauline and family and Mark, Ruth and Alan. She used Eri's Meissen china for the first time.

December 16, 1981—Nancy, Jim, Mark, Ruth and Alan will come on Sunday for Jim and Nancy's 25th wedding anniversary at Ginny and Jerry's house. They will have dinner at Neil's house on Sunday. I will try to go.
**Neil had a tasty meal and then we went to Ginny's for the afternoon. A photographer was hired, and a number of family photographs were taken of my mother with her grandchildren and great-grandchildren.*

December 29, 1981—Neil and I were to Jerry and Ginny's for Christmas dinner. It was nice to see the tree, gifts and the kids with their toys and games. It was a lovely, frosty-tree day like a picture post card.

Diary Entries 1982

February 1, 1982—Mary was here on Saturday morning with the new baby. There is no name for her yet and she's two weeks old. She is a pretty baby.

**There was some discussion over the naming of her, but in the end Kaisa prevailed. Some individuals said the name was too unusual and would be difficult to spell or pronounce correctly. Others said the school children would use it as a means to make jokes and taunt her. And still others said it was an old country name and not suitable for an American child. As time went on, most everyone came to realize that Kaisa was most suitable. Mary chose Elizabeth for her second name. Kaisa and Elizabeth were compatible and rolled off the tongue with the greatest of ease.

February 14, 1982—Neil took me to Mary and Lou's. The baby was baptized Kaisa Elizabeth Efta.

February 22, 1982—Neil came this afternoon and brought along a centennial button for the Alma Township celebration. There is a picture of the old school house on it. Nancy and Jim were here and brought a watercolor of our old home that Nancy painted. She also painted the Brosdahl and Jorgenson homes. She painted them for the Alma Township centennial.

March 8, 1982—Neil is getting excited about the Alma Township centennial because he is in charge of ordering the food for the free dinner.

March 14, 1982—Jerry leaves for South America to be gone three weeks. He was chosen to go to South America and Mexico to sell wheat as a member of the wheat board. I hate to see him go on this trip. He flies from Grand Forks into Mexico City.

April 7, 1982—Neil took Ginny and family to the airport on Sunday to meet Jerry. I haven't seen him yet.

April 12, 1982—Jerry showed us his slides. They were interesting scenes. We saw his llama rug. It is very lovely. It is black and white. He gave me a white wool scarf.

**Jerry most likely forgot that Mother could not tolerate wool next to her skin. Perhaps that particular scarf was made of softer, not so itchy wool.

April 14, 1982—Neil took me to the clinic at Warren to see about glasses and the bruise on my leg. I will get glasses in two weeks. My eyes hadn't changed much. The bruise may open—so Dr. Pumela says.

April 22, 1982—Ivan read sixty books for the March of Dimes and made $42 for them.

April 24, 1982—It is eighty-two above this afternoon. Neil was here yesterday. They'll begin field work soon.

May 3, 1982—We had a thunder shower last night. The grass is green.

May 7, 1982—The bus took me to the hospital where I had fifteen stitches in my leg that I hurt on Easter Sunday. Jerry went to the hospital with viral pneumonia. He had a 103 fever.

May 8, 1982—Nancy came and stopped awhile. She brought the painting she did of the "Old House." She gave it to me for a Mother's Day gift.

**I had just started painting in watercolor with community education classes from Ellen Eilers in Alexandria. Later I drove to Grand Rapids, Minnesota, and took several weeklong watercolor classes from Edgar E. Whitney. He had a great influence on my work.

May 11, 1982—The handyman put up the painting of the "Old House." It looks nice.

May 21, 1982—I went to the doctor to have him look at my leg. I will go back on Monday or Tuesday to get the stitches out.

May 31, 1982—Neil said they had one hundred acres to seed yet.

June 2, 1982—Nancy writes that their neighbor, Johnny Elvehjem, died of a heart attack. Jim is to be a pallbearer.

**Johnny's daughter Joyce missed her "PaPa", and said that Jim might fill in for him.

June 8, 1982—Neil was here. It rained two inches at the farm on Tuesday. The crops look good. They have one hundred acres of buckwheat yet to plant. They will sell it to Japan.

June 14, 1982—Selma died last night. I saw her at suppertime in the hall. She died in her room. The nurses were with her. Her sister, Esther Hansen, and her daughters and husband were here this afternoon. Her funeral is from the Baptist church on Tuesday at 2:00 p.m.

**Selma was a widow who lived across from the Schey School with her brother, Willie Wallin. Sometimes the teacher roomed with her during the school year. Mother, Dad and Neil took both Selma and Willie

under their wings, driving them to appointments, visiting them, and having them as guests for meals. Their lovely yard with its huge trees became the site where Lou and Mary Efta built their house.

JULY 5, 1982—We had a big storm. It came up about 9:30. The nurses took us all out in the hall—me in a nightgown. Later on they got me a blanket. We were out of our rooms about an hour. It rained hard from—from two inches to ten inches in the North.

JULY 10, 1982—Nancy came with the paintings and two books. She left a painting of the "Old School" and took the one of the "Old House" to show at the Alma Township centennial.

JULY 11, 1982—It was the Alma Township picnic. (It was held at the Schey School, which by that time was a town hall). Many people came. Neil took the Winnebago and parked it under a tree on the grounds. I sat in it and a number of people came in it to visit me. They were: Edna Brosdahl, Anna Thorson, Gerda Moe, Doris Bagaas, Helen Herseth, Betty Rantanen, Donna, Armand and Heather Westlund, Lloyd Cole and Elizabeth Johnson. Nancy sold three paintings. She had them outside (on a display rack).
**This was a major event in the life of the small community of Alma Township. It was memorable in many ways. I had my paintings there, which were of local subjects. Mother held court in the Winnebago. Many people came from a distance, and the Schey cabin was open for people to view.*

JULY 17, 1982—Arne is working in the gold mines in Alaska.

JULY 23, 1982—Heather was Jr. Style Queen at the Marshall County fair.
**Heather won a crown and a monetary award.*

JULY 24, 1982—Pete Stanko (one of the residents) came into my room last night at midnight. I was scared. I yelled until the nurse came and took him (away) from the room.
**Danger can be lurking in the most unexpected of places.*

AUGUST 2, 1982—Mary's baby (Kaisa) creeps now.

AUGUST 5, 1982—Mary and children were here in the morning. They are trying to make hay and it rains nearly every day.

AUGUST 9, 1982—Neil took me for a ride east on Sunday. There was quite a bit of grain in the swath. The boys got the rye combined. The sunflowers are in blossom.

AUGUST 17, 1982—Mary and her family of six were here in the morning. Joe wheeled me to dinner. Everyone followed along (behind). Kaisa looked cute sitting on my lap.
**This must have seemed like a parade to the other residents.*

AUGUST 28, 1982—Arne (Rantanen) got a job near Anchorage building roads.

SEPTEMBER 4, 1982—Nancy and Jim came in the morning. She brought me the "Old House" painting.

SEPTEMBER 5, 1982—Neil took me out home for dinner and the afternoon. Nancy and Ginny made the dinner. Nancy made an apple pie and we had escalloped potatoes with hamburger, new beets and buns.

SEPTEMBER 15, 1982—Harriet and her husband and Roy and wife (the Wood family) sat with Mabel until 10 P.M. They thought she would die but she is still alive.

SEPTEMBER 20, 1982—Jerry was here with Meredith. She was so cute in a red pinafore.

SEPTEMBER 22, 1982—Mabel (Wood) died on Tuesday morning. The funeral is on the 23rd. My new roommate is Elizabeth Hillman.
**Life is as fragile as a snowflake. Death comes on its own schedule, not ours.*

OCTOBER 4, 1982—Neil took me for a ride to the east and south. The sunflowers hang their heads, but the trees were still bright yellow in places.

OCTOBER 8, 1982—When we got back to the room from the birthdays—a new clock was on the wall. I thought Neil brought it but then found out it was Mrs. Hillman's sons who put it up. Neil also came a bit later with a clock. I thought this very funny.

OCTOBER 11, 1982—Neil got a satellite dish and gets twenty stations on it. He had a group of friends to see it in the evening.

OCTOBER 21, 1982—Ruth got a job with a glass company in the Twin Cities. She is in public relations.

OCTOBER 22, 1982—Neil was here and said they began to combine corn today. The leaves are mostly gone.

OCTOBER 27, 1982—The third grade had a party for us. Garth was in the program. They did Halloween skits and dances. Garth was a vampire with a cape and horns on his head. He came and talked to me and kissed me on leaving.

NOVEMBER 4, 1982—Rudy Perpich was elected governor of the state of Minnesota.

NOVEMBER 5, 1982—I didn't vote because I would have needed to take the bus to the fire-hall.
**Evidentially, absentee voting wasn't taking place at that time. Mother clearly wanted to vote, having done so for the first time in 1920.*

NOVEMBER 11, 1982—Donna and Armand (Westlund) stopped on their way back home from Fargo. Donna got the Golden Circle Award for caring for a boy two years old and his mother who had cancer.

NOVEMBER 25, 1982—Neil took me to Betty's for Thanksgiving dinner. It was a lovely day.

DECEMBER 6, 1982—Nancy and Jim came up December 3ʳᵈ in the morning and left on the 4ᵗʰ after lunch. I was out to the new house to have walleye to eat.

DECEMBER 16, 1982—I got four Christmas cards. One of them was from Laura Borg of Los Angeles, California.
*Later on, I came to know her son Hugo and daughter Alice. I flew to Los Angeles and met them. He brought his family photographs for me to see and help identify. Laura Borg was my mother's second cousin and the daughter of Vine Tuffs Smith.

DECEMBER 25, 1982—Neil and I were at Jerry and Ginny's for dinner. It was a feast.

DECEMBER 29, 1981—"It was a lovely frosty tree day like a picture post card."
*This entry epitomizes Ruth's attitude toward life. Countless entries begin with the two-word statement, "lovely day." As I read the diaries, she presents an image of reason and resolve. She reports the daily happenings of her life as they were, accepting her limitations and losses without rancor. As her physical condition worsened, her mental capacity held steady. Her diaries end in 1982. She died May 3, 1987, having written her last letter to me three days earlier.

Postscript

My fascination with family history began in childhood. I loved listening to my mother's stories of the Matthews and the wooden box that came with her in the covered wagon. This wooden box contained tintypes of a youthful couple—the woman held flowers and the man was dressed in a suit. I puzzled over their identity. The woman was so lovely and the man distinguished. One day an idea occurred to me to compare the tintypes to another photograph. The two couples had enough similarities—especially the beards on both men—to connect them. And then it hit me, "These tintypes are wedding portraits of Jacob Matthews and Nancy Powers (Matthews) from October 17, 1844. Oh my goodness, I have found my ancestors!" I exalted.

This sudden knowledge coursed through my system like an electric current, catapulting me into action—my German resolve firmly in place! What would have been a most difficult project was accomplished with relative ease due to the invaluable contributions of both the living and dead. It is in this manner that Lovely Day has become a reality.

—Nancy Kruger Olson

About the Author

Nancy Kruger Olson has been a visual artist for thirty years, working in watercolor, pastel and woodcuts. In 2000 she published *We Flew With Our Own Wings*. She is listed in several "Who's Who" publications: *Midwest*, the *World*, *America*, *Education and Women*.

She became a member of the Daughters of the American Revolution in 2003 by using her Matthews lineage as documentation.

Nancy lives with her husband James in a rustic, light-filled "Danish Cabin" with a view of earth and sky.